WILL YOU WALK INTO MY PARLOUR?

CW01498503

DENARII PETERS

Crystal
Clear
Books

First Published in Great Britain by Crystal Clear Books 2024

Published by: Crystal Clear Books: www.crystalclearbooks.co.uk

ISBN: 978-1-7394272-6-9

Cover Image: Mystic Art Design, Pixabay

One day Steve Battley said to me, "*Why don't you write your stories down?*" So I did. And here they are.

ACKNOWLEDGEMENTS

Where do I start? I've so many people to thank.

Jenni, my alpha beta reader extraordinaire, always ready to peruse another version. Sue, my editor, spotter of the missing comma; mistress of the semicolon. Linda, my publisher: thanks again for the opportunity, Liz for her super photograph, Kate for her enthusiasm, Sandra for her support and Chris for his lovely veg. Also, the members of the Horncastle creative writing group, who sat patiently through early readings. Then there are all the lovely judges of the short story and flash fiction competitions in which some of these tales have won, placed or been highly commended.

But most of all I have to thank my husband, for putting up with the tantrums ("That doesn't work." "Why doesn't the computer work?"), the strange hours (Have I really been writing since 5.30 am?), the credit he refuses to take for pointing out the glaring errors. And, of course, the coffee. (It doesn't make itself.) Quite simply, without his support, there would be no book.

Denarii Peters
https://denariipeters.substack.com/
July 2024.

STORIES PREVIOUSLY PUBLISHED:

Soaking Wet was first published in 2023 by Crystal Clear Books in the anthology Hysteria 10, edited by Linda Parkinson-Hardman.

All That Remains was first published in 2024 by the Scottish Arts Trust on their website.

Just A Little Deeper was first published in 2023 by Beagle North in the anthology Halloween: 13 Tales of Terror, edited by Rebecca Panks and Jack Bumby.

A Basket of Peonies was first published in 2023 by The Anansi Archive in the anthology Find Me Here, edited by Dave Jordan.

How To Murder A Ghost was first published in 2023 by Hobeck Books in the anthology Henshaw Five, edited by Rebecca Collins.

Golden Apple Inc. was first published in 2023 by The Norwich Writers' Circle in the anthology Telling Tales, edited by Iain Andrews.

Lime Tree Arbour was first published in 2022 by The Anansi Archive in the anthology Show Me Where It Hurts, edited by Dave Jordan.

The Unkindness of Witches was first published in 2023 by Hobeck Books in the anthology Henshaw Five, edited by Rebecca Collins.

Perchance To Dream was first published in 2024 by The Anansi Archive in the anthology Spider, edited by Dave Jordan.

CONTENTS

WILL YOU WALK INTO MY PARLOUR?

It's an old road, a cold road, a forgotten, not-even-on-Google-maps road. What possessed them to move out here "off the grid" I will never know. When I started out this morning, driving through the fens in the bright sunshine of an early autumn day, it felt like an adventure. It doesn't feel like one now.

It was a long drive. I should have had more sense than to attempt it when I knew my vehicle was in such bad shape.

I stopped for lunch in a small village: nothing more than a sprawling set of farm buildings, half a dozen houses and a creepy, old, ivy covered inn. I was hungry but there was nowhere else in sight. A painted sign gave notice that locally produced, hand reared ham and free range egg pies were the speciality of the house. The hostelry was called The Gargoyle and the object leered at me from above the low lintel. It looked like it had been stolen from an ancient church. Beneath it was an inscription in flowing letters; not the name of the landlord but a bit of rubbish doggerel:

"The runner can be the flier's dinner,
The scrabbler can be the swimmer's tea
But the one who walks in darkness to the candle,

That one belongs to me."

I meant to ask the landlord why he had such strange words written above his door (they did not strike me as welcoming) but somehow I forgot.

There were several people at the bar and more dotted at tables round the room. No one was eating any kind of pie. I picked up the menu. No pie there either.

"There's a shortage o' ham. I'm waitin' for some comin' in. Why not try the fish and chips, eh?"

I didn't want fish and chips but it was too much effort to argue.

Half an hour later I was back in the car. In response to the landlord's probing I had told him where I was headed. He suggested a short cut which, he said, "Takes miles off the journey, though it's a bit narrower. You have to watch out for the tractors, mind, and do make sure you stay on the road. These 'ere parts can be a bit tricky at night."

It sounded like a good idea. The road couldn't be any worse than the one which had brought me to the inn. Every second driver had been a snail crawling along, no doubt not going far and not in any hurry to get there. However, before long I was wondering if I had not made a mistake. The "road" was nothing more than a cart track with only a handful of passing places. There were deep ditches on either side, reminders that all this was reclaimed land and well deserved the name South Holland.

Soon dusk was falling and the landscape was too flat, the sky too wide. I was impatient for the journey to be over.

Perhaps I lost concentration, lulled by the unending road as it snaked through the fields, curve upon curve for no reason I could see. Why didn't it go in a straight line? There were no hills to skirt, no obstacles of any kind.

Out of nowhere I was facing a huge, agricultural beast of a tractor. The dingy brown cab was splattered with thick mud and had garish bright yellow equipment strapped to the front consisting of a tangle of painted metal pipes and what looked a bit like large plastic flower buds. It came at me going far too fast for the track we were on, leaving me with nowhere to go, no passing place, no way to pull aside. The man in the cab was coming at me as if I wasn't there, as if he were alone on a wide and empty road. I attempted to give him space, one wheel then another on the verge, yet still there wasn't enough room for him to get by me.

With a sickening lurch the car slid sideways over the slippery grass and down into the drainage ditch. For a second I was too shocked to move. Then I realised the passenger side of the vehicle was still sinking. I threw open my door and managed to scramble out.

My feet were soaking since the grass was only a thin covering on top of sticky, waterlogged ground. I stumbled away from the car. There was nothing I could do, no way to get it out of the ditch without help.

I tried to lean back inside to retrieve my jacket with my phone in the pocket but I couldn't reach it and the car rocked as it sank a little deeper. It was too dangerous. I had to leave it.

I stared down the road in the direction the tractor had been heading. It was no longer in sight. One too many twists in the track had removed it from my view. I couldn't believe the driver had continued on his journey. Hadn't he realised he had driven me off the road?

I was left with few options. The sky was becoming ever darker and there was only a sliver of moonlight. I could not stay where I was. It would soon be cold enough for frost. I had to find shelter and help. At least I was on a track which, according to the landlord, did lead somewhere.

I tramped along the rough surface for what seemed like hours, tired and so very cold. Why were there no cars on this road if it was a recognised shortcut? By now my friends would be wondering what had happened to me but it was too soon for them to become alarmed. In any case, if they did go in search of me, they would look in the obvious place, along the main road. No one would expect to find me here in the midst of the fens.

What was that? A light in the distance? Could it be a farm? If I stayed on the road, I would get there eventually but it looked much quicker to cut across the fields.

I found a small bridge over the drainage ditch, no doubt a path for tractors to use while harvesting, and started off across the stubbly remnants of the crop. At first there was a clear track but moments later it petered out and I was surrounded by empty fields filled with darkening shadows. The ground, which had appeared so flat from the driving seat of my moving car, had given way to humps of turned mud and clumps of tall stalks.

I began to panic. I stumbled across the rough ground, shouting, calling out for someone, anyone to help me as I struggled to fight back my rising terror.

There was no answering shout. All I heard was the hoot of an owl and the soft sigh of a twilight breeze.

Now, as I set off across the endless, flat fields, hundreds of dying sunflowers dip their heads, twisting towards me in slow motion. In the failing light they are as threatening as a wasteland of triffids. Small, fearful bundles of fur skitter between the stalks while overhead a pure white shadow invades the silence with the cry of an ancient ghost.

I shiver as, with a scream, the mouse is caught in the talons of the owl: the runner becoming the flyer's dinner.

Beside me a splash in the cold, dark channel of field drained water, the sides sticky with fenland mud. I cannot say whether it is deep or shallow but I know there is no purchase, no trailing root for a claw to grasp to find a way back out.

Unable to help, I walk away as behind me a shrew is clamped in an otter's jaws: the scrabbler becoming the swimmer's tea.

I see again the gargoyle's inscription. Surely two small deaths should be enough. But my steps are heavy with a terror I cannot name.

Ahead of me, against the sky, is not a farm at all but the sails of a long abandoned windmill and, inside the building, a flickering light as though from a guttering candle. But I cannot go much further. I am lost, afraid, becoming too cold at the end of a night now threatening frost. Do I go inside?

Do I have a choice?

SOAKING WET

I never did like it when they came in threes. Even when my heart was happy it was too much work. All that torturing and drowning. And when the situation was like this...

I tried again to be heard. I was supposed to be in charge. I was the one who could tell if the accused was a servant of the devil or a foolish old crone. It was my decision to try by water or destroy by fire.

"Sit down. Stop shouting. Everyone will get their chance to speak. But it must be one at a time. Otherwise how can my clerk possibly list all your accusations?"

"They're not accusations. They're true."

A rumble of agreement followed the baker's words. He was a bruiser, arms as thick as his head. And one of the three was his own wife! She was not the one who had caught my eye though.

"We're wasting time. We brought you here to burn 'em." He was playing to the gallery, enjoying the moment, his wife too frightened even to sob let alone protest her innocence. And I had seen enough women exactly like her to know she was indeed innocent. I wondered which of the other women in the crowd the baker had chosen to take her place in his bed.

It was time I cleared the room; time for the charade to begin. I nodded to my clerk and Simon got to his feet.

"The Witchfinder is ready to start. He will give his verdicts in two days' time. You will all disperse and leave this to us."

Grumbling, they shuffled out. They had hoped for more: a bit of blood, a request for tinder. But they didn't need to be so impatient. They would not be disappointed. All that would follow sure enough.

The baker's wife collapsed into the arms of her companions. Perhaps she had thought he would relent when he saw me, realise it had all gone too far. If so, she had clung to a false hope.

I gave her to Simon, so enthusiastic, so eager for a victim of his own. He had not yet discovered the trade of the torturer is a boring occupation.

And, what was worse still, he was now becoming suspicious of me. He was watching my every move and if I were to make a misstep along the way, give him the slightest cause, he would not hesitate to denounce me. If burning a "witch" gave pleasure to the mob, burning a witchfinder corrupted by the devil would give them ecstasy.

All had been well between us until a couple of months ago when we were summoned to a small village and a smaller child. She was no more than seven. Her grandmother was the one on trial but, as is often the case, one burning is never enough. The child had the mark of a dog bite on her leg: those around her claimed it was the mark of the devil. There was nothing I could do. I could not save her. The mob would have come for me if I had tried.

When I went to sleep that night I saw her eyes; not accusing but terrified. My nightmare became a parade of horror, filled with the faces of those I had condemned over the five years of my tenure. Not all had been women. There was the young man who had shouted defiance from the midst of the flames… until his cries became howls. He had taken a long time to die. I knew why. The villagers had steeped some of the tinder in water so that around his body it did not burn but only smouldered: more heat, less flame.

I had become a hollow shell, too afraid to stand up; too afraid to leave my robes behind; too afraid of the accusations which could be levelled against me. So I continued to do the work. But with every false verdict I found the words more difficult and every night I suffered my own torture.

Now there was this young woman, her hair the same raven black, her eyes the same deep green as the girl in the village. They could have been mother and daughter. Would it end my nightmares if I could find a way save her?

Simon's interrogation of the baker's wife went awry. She died by his hand but the mob tied her to the stake and burned her anyway. The other two verdicts could not be delayed much longer. I decided we should swim them.

Tied hand and foot, gagged to prevent the speaking of spells, they would be thrown into the river. If they drowned, they'd be given a Christian funeral. If they floated, they'd be dried out then burned.

I saw to the knots myself. Risking everything, I whispered into her ear, "The rope is slack. Wriggle free but do not surface. Swim as far as you can underwater. I will distract the mob."

She held still as I tied the same loose knots on the other woman. But my plan for her was different.

Into the water, thrown from the bridge, shouts obscuring the splashes… I knew what would happen. It is human to struggle. My accusing finger pointed to the floating rope and the choking victim. The plan worked. No one looked for the one who surely must have drowned. Her innocence would be her reward; an early entry into Heaven.

I'll leave Simon to take care of the drying and the burning. I've done my duty and someone has to see if it's possible to gather the corpse from the water.

Racing away downstream, I look for her long, dark hair. She can't have swum far but there is no sign of her. The banks are silent; the thick reed beds undisturbed.

I stumble on, blinded by tears. I have failed. Something must have gone wrong with my knots. She has indeed died and I have once again murdered innocence.

But out in the stream there are ripples; small eddies with no current; a whirlpool. She springs from the water, soaking wet but so very alive.

Calling out strange words, she opens her arms to me. We rise up above the river and as we fly away from the village I realise the truth.

Only a witch cannot drown.

ALL THAT REMAINS

I am temptation, an illicit thrill, the old witch's last and greatest creation. Come closer. See how I sparkle: iridescent green, purple, blue. Inside this tiny bottle I could be a dragon held suspended or merely oil on water.

That's right. Take me in your hand. Hold me to your eye. What do you see? Floating fragments of precious metals, crushed rubies and emeralds, all of them changing, flowing, coalescing.

What am I? What did she bring into being with her mixture of blood and herbs gathered on a cold midnight beneath the full moon? Could I bind your lover or destroy your enemies? Will I bring you wealth or end all your hopes?

There is only one way to find out and that is not to replace me on the high, dusty shelf for another to discover.

You came in here to seek anything she might have left behind, bringing with you the reek of her burning flesh. You would have been her apprentice if she had let you. So yes, you could be right. I may be meant for you alone.

I am all the magic that remains in this place. There are no incantations for you to take away, no books in a sealed chest. She never did learn to write.

So what am I? Her final gift or her final curse? It all depends on what she knew, on whether or not she guessed the one who betrayed her...

...was you.

JUST A LITTLE DEEPER

"What do you think you're doing?"

I spin round, only just missing my foot with the spade. I stare up at the woman who has emerged from the other side of the tangled brambles. How she got here I can't imagine. There's not a scratch on her or her clothing and she looks as if she's come from a fancy party or maybe a wedding. But I know there's been nothing on here today. There are no events planned at all for the this week or next. It's the quiet season. But here she is with her long cream skirt trailing through the scattered twigs and leaf litter. No sign of any clubs either, but then not even the most ardent golfer would be out on the course in the dark on a night like this.

Before she arrived everything had been going so well. I made sure I would be alone. I double checked to make certain there wasn't a single vehicle left in the car park and every light in the clubhouse was out.

The night itself is starless, the moon hidden by the heavy clouds. The ground is soft since there has been more than enough rain in the last few days. Until now things were looking up after the unhappy events earlier in the evening.

"Is that a grave you're digging?" With the toe of her boot she nudges the heap of soil I have removed in order to create this deep rectangle in the damp, red streaked clay. "Is it for that man lying over there?"

It's as though we're engaging in a game of twenty questions, not one of which I am prepared to answer. But then, do I need to explain what I'm up to? She has eyes, hasn't she? Can't she work it out? This muddy hole beneath the trees in the rough to one side of the thirteenth hole didn't get here by itself, did it? And no way am I here in the middle of the night on a clandestine hunt for buried treasure.

"Who was he, the man you killed?"

"Does it matter? You wouldn't have known him anyway. He was a rather unpleasant sort when all's said and done."

"Is that the reason you killed him, just because he was unpleasant?"

Why is she so curious? Hasn't it dawned on her she might be in danger herself? If I had been in her boots, I would have been streaking my way over the greens, trying to find help, not taking the risk of asking obvious questions of an obvious murderer.

"I didn't intend to kill him. It was an accident."

"An accident, eh? Oh, that makes it all right, then, doesn't it? Well, I suppose I'd better let you get on with what you're doing. It's been ever so nice talking to you. Bye!"

As she walks past me I realise I can't let her leave. She's seen too much. The first thing she'll do will be go to the police station only a few streets away and tell them what she has found me doing. One sniff of my description and, what with my record...

I don't give myself any more time to think. I pick the spade up out of the hole and whirl it through the air. I smash it into the side of her head.

She falls in slow motion, a pale, white cloud with long, dark hair cartwheeling into a preprepared grave that was never dug for her. There ought to be a tide of blood spurting out of a deep wound drenching me and the clay. But there isn't. She ought to be unconscious. But she isn't.

Lying on her back, she wags a finger at me. "What did you do that for? It wasn't very friendly, was it?"

For an instant I want to laugh. This situation is now so ridiculous I have to be dreaming it. Everything is all right. I didn't murder Jonathan Livermore earlier in the evening. I didn't climb in through his first storey window using a rickety ladder taken from his garage. I didn't bash his brains in with the decorative fake Victorian poker which he keeps beside his fake coal fire. Yes, I am in my bed having a nightmare, that's all. In the morning I will wake up and laugh about it.

Ah but, no. All this is real. Too real. I can't have hit her hard enough. I'll have to have another go.

But before I can raise the spade she's on her feet. There isn't a speck of mud on the long, cream skirt or the crisp white blouse, not a mark on her face or her neck, not a cut, not a bruise of any kind.

My fingers suddenly numb, the spade falls through them and squelches onto the ground beside me.

"Well, answer me. Why did you do it? Anyone would think you wanted to kill me too and that would be a silly waste of time, wouldn't it?"

"I'm sorry. I must have hurt you."

"Nah, not really. It was a weird sensation, though, like the first time I walked through a wall."

"You're a ghost?" Stupid question! What else could she be?

"I think you ought to get on with what you were doing. It's not nice for him lying out in the open like that, going cold, getting stiff."

"No, I suppose it isn't." I can't bring myself to pick up the spade again. My hands are trembling too much.

She steps out of the hole. It's not difficult. It only comes up to her knees. "I'd say this should be more than twice as deep. What do you think?" She isn't talking to me. She's looking over my shoulder at something behind me.

I hear a deep, guttural cough. "I agree. I think it should be at least twice as deep as that and maybe a bit longer too. I was nearly six foot, you know."

My mouth is dry. I'm fixed to the spot.

The gruff voice of Jonathan Livermore continues, "It's bad enough being cut off in your prime by some weasly little oik who's broken in to steal your favourite painting. Now it looks as if I'm going to have to suffer the indignity of not being able to lie straight and, what's worse, risk being dug up by some silly spaniel out in search of golf balls."

I don't dare move a muscle. This cannot be happening.

"Well, get on with it. Pick up that confounded shovel and..." Jonathan Livermore walks round me, a patch of freezing air ruffling my hair as he does so. He points to the spade. "That's mine too, isn't it? Not content with killing me, you steal my best gardening equipment into the bargain!"

"I had to. You know I live in a top floor flat. I don't have a garden so why would I own a spade?"

"Is that where you were planning to hang my painting? In your pokey, little garret? What a waste of fine art."

"No, I'm going to sell it. I have a fence lined up and waiting."

"The joke's on you, then, you idiot. The thing's a fake. And not even a good one. It only cost me seventy quid."

"I'm not sure it was that good a bargain. It did get you killed, didn't it?" He might be a ghost but he's still the same annoying prat I've known and hated since we were kids at school. "If I dig you a nice, extra deep grave, will that shut you up?"

"Maybe. It would certainly help. But it would have to be a decent depth. I won't settle for anything less." He and the woman both laugh as he thrusts his face into mine. "In fact, I won't settle at all. I'll haunt you instead."

"All right." I step into the hole and with the sharp edge of the stolen spade I begin to remove another few centimetres. Digging is hard work and I have been here too long already. But I don't want to be haunted. "Will this do?"

"Are you kidding? Have you never been to a burial? You've still got a long way to go. You're not even half way yet." Jonathan breathes icy air into the trench. "Tell you what. I'll sweeten it for you. When you've got it just right I'll tell you where I stashed the real painting."

"You do have it, then?"

"I've got more than just that one. And I can't take them with me, can I? Put your back into it, man. It's starting to rain. My corpse is getting wet."

I dig and I dig and I dig. The top of the hole is now level with my shoulders.

"That'll do. You can stop now. Chuck the spade out."

I'm not thinking. I do as he says. I'm too exhausted and too relieved it's over. I'm dreaming about going and getting the painting, the real painting, the one that's worth a fortune. I'll be rich. I'll be...

But the soil crumbles under my fingers. I can see the spade just out of reach. I scrabble at the sides of the hole but there's nothing to cling on to. The rain is pouring now, cascading down. My legs give way and I slither into the liquid mud. I can't see anything. My mouth, caught in a scream, fills with earth and I'm so tired, while all I can hear is two ghosts above me on firm ground laughing as they prepare to welcome one more.

OH HELL

They've had problems with me from the moment I first arrived but, no matter what they say, I have every right to be here. This is the one place I do belong and, although I didn't know it when I was young, I had been fighting to get here every day of my life.

I'm not unique. There are quite a few like me. We recognise each other by that certain look in the eyes, that tight smile and those many scars displayed out in the open like badges identifying us as members of a proud and disreputable cult.

When I finally did reach this place, after such a long journey, after so many difficulties, I realised I had spent my whole life as an outcast living in a place where no one even came close to understanding me. My ways were not the same as those of the people around me. Labels were attached to me. As a child the name calling caused me pain but as I grew older so I grew into those names. I stole them by making them mine and on occasion threw them back.

Yes, that is what I am. Want to make something of it? Hey, don't run away. I haven't hurt you yet. Don't you want me to prove I am what you say I am: alien, strange, different?

Well, I was never happy. Always restless, I knew I was missing something. Life had to be more interesting and I remember the weather was always too cold, always raining, never warm and sunny. I dreamt of heat, of waking every day under a hot sun.

At fifteen I stole my first car, got caught and was cautioned.

"Naughty, little joyrider," said the police officer. "If you don't mend your ways, my girl, you'll end up somewhere you don't want to be."

"Where would that be, then?"

He narrowed his eyes and strode off. He didn't think I deserved a reply.

By seventeen I had become the getaway driver for a gang of robbers. Perfect at it, I was. No one suspects a pretty girl sitting in a car. She's obviously waiting for the boyfriend. We got away with a nice, little string of jobs... until the lads didn't get out of the bank in time and I waited too long for them. Took a suspicious policewoman to notice me. Three male coppers just walked right on past.

So I was sent to prison for the next couple of years. Sweet. And I was up with the system. Never had it so good. Bullies always fit in. Shame the authorities didn't take my bad behaviour into account because they released me early. My brief (well, my parents' brief; I didn't ask for him) told the court, "Prison is doing this young woman no good. She is being influenced by the wrong people. If she is given parole now, there is a chance she will reform and become a well adjusted member of society. Leave her any longer and I fear we will lose our opportunity. She will become institutionalised and we will be looking at her pattern of antisocial behaviour becoming ingrained."

No one asked my opinion. So they opened the gates and threw me out.

The next three years flew by. In certain circles I got the reputation of leading a charmed life. "Take Addie on the job and you won't get caught." Not my fault. I was just always in the wrong place at the wrong time with the wrong crew. I was a brilliant getaway driver and there wasn't a car I couldn't get into in less that twenty seconds from a standing start. Trouble was, give me someone on my tail, I would automatically go faster and faster and they would always lose the pursuit. Anyone would think I hadn't enjoyed my time behind bars. I suppose I could have gone into a police station and shouted, "It was me! I did that bank heist." But I'm no snitch.

One day I got invited to help with a little job at an art gallery and for once I was on the inside, not driving the car. Not my usual style at all. But I was glad they did ask me because that was where I saw the only piece of art that has ever appealed to me. You could say it even helped shape the rest of my life. It wasn't the picture we'd come for, wasn't even on the wall. It was on the cover of a book in the gallery shop. I stared at it, pressed my nose to the window for a closer look, even forgot all about fingerprints as I placed my hands on the glass.

"Come on, Addie! We've gotta go. Something's triggered the effing alarm." Phil and the others raced past me but I wanted that book so much I didn't care about the bells ringing all round us. Phil had to drag me away.

It took ages to track the image down. Turns out I wasn't looking in the right places. Hieronymus Bosch's *Hell* was no holiday poster. What a shame. I had to accept there was no way I could book a trip. What a pity. But at least now I knew where I wanted to end up. All I had to do was be bad enough to secure my place in the Inferno.

For many long years I did my best. I was forever in and out of prisons. A judge about to sentence me once joked, "Ms. Lister, I suspect you are attempting to collect a fridge magnet from every one of his majesty's establishments of incarceration. Well, don't let me be the one to scupper your endeavour."

I could have told him some were more fun than others. Perhaps I should have gone into the guide book business and started my own rating system: one star for those boring places where they keep a watchful eye on you, five for the ones where I spent most time in solitary for hurting. And getting hurt. I never could decide which I preferred.

The authorities tried everything to reform me but none of them even came close. I had a strong dislike in particular for the religious types, like the priest I saw who once told me, "God will forgive you, my dear. His grace is there for all."

"Oh no, not me. I'm destined for Hell."

"Don't say that. There is always hope."

"I am hoping!" I was. But not in the way he meant.

And so the day came. I was driving too fast. As always. I skidded on a patch of oil and went straight over a cliff, just like in the movies. I couldn't have asked for a more appropriate exit: from the heat of a blazing car into the blazing heat of the Inferno.

And at first Hell was just like I hoped it would be, so like the Bosch images. I always knew the painting was an advert for the place. This was where I belonged; the ultimate haven for a violent, vicious, sadomasochistic harmer, both of herself and of others.

But it wasn't to last.

Today, when I go outside, everything has changed. All my scars have vanished. When I open my mouth I'm unable to say anything unpleasant. Everyone is smiling at me and I can't seem to summon up the energy to hurt any of them. There's nothing worth stealing and there aren't even any cars.

This place is more like a Heaven than a Hell and I can't stand it. It's not what I signed up for. It seems they've at last found a solution to the problem of how to punish a paradise hating Hell-cat.

Oh, Hell. Please let me out! I don't belong here!

THE OTHER SIDE OF ETERNITY

Every day we discard the bodies. The dead would pile up if we left them where they fell. The stench of decaying flesh would make for a less than pleasant working environment. If we were ever to come to the end of our task (not, of course, that such an outcome is possible) we would be faced with endless fields of graves. Or, maybe, so much time would have passed that the shifting continents of the Earth will have covered them with a new mountain range or fossilised them under a new sea. This always assumes we are on Earth and the stories we tell our children are not mere legends given birth by our own fears and those of our forebears; fears of being rootless, stateless, even world-less. For all we know, we could be the homeless of the universe and this unending construction project the equivalent of a cardboard box under a bridge.

My grandfather told me the tales his grandfather had told him of how in days gone by this structure only reached the height of a worker's knees. We are doing well. There is progress even here for now the wall is more than a hand's breadth higher than that.

Sometimes my memory plays tricks on me and for a few seconds I believe it was once as tall as my shoulders. But the notion is so foolish I dare not even suggest it as a joke to my fellow workers.

The architect is picky and his clients even more so. They are in no hurry to take up residence. They require perfection and the positioning of only one brick in a million meets their exacting standards. I have never succeeded in pleasing them nor has anyone I know but someone must have or this great hall would still only be a traced outline or its cornerstone would stand in splendid isolation.

I have never encountered the architect nor do I hope to. His last visit is recorded on paper so ancient it has become our most precious artefact. I know there are a few among us who do not believe he ever came at all but they must be wrong. If there was no visit, how could the progress we have made have been checked and measured? If there were no architect and, by extension, no clients, our work would be worthless and our existence would be futile.

Beyond the wall there is nothingness. How could there be anything else? As children we are taught not to gaze out into the thick, endless grey that begins a footfall outside the line of our construction. Those who do not heed the wise words of their elders go insane. They swear they can see all sorts of shapes in the shifting mists. Perhaps they are right. Somewhere there must be a stockpile of bricks, new bricks to replace the ones we have used, the ones we have managed to place in a precise enough line, the ones that do not vanish from the construction during the time we sleep.

There are a few gaps in the wall wide enough to step through. Were this place to ever be finished, it is believed they will become the doorways. For now they are the exits through which we push the bodies of those who have just died and the entrances through which our bread and water appear. We must eat or we will die before new workers can be born, can grow and can be made ready to take our places. In the ancient legends there is foolish talk of different foods with strange names but most of us do not believe they ever existed. If they did, they would have been part of a different life and everyone knows this is the only life there has ever been or ever will be.

Something strange has happened today. My friend, who has always worked beside me and sometimes used to speak words I did not understand (blasphemies based on forbidden tales and a misunderstanding of our purpose) has disappeared. He was not at breakfast. No one has seen him all morning. As I begin to smooth new mortar on top of the one brick still standing from yesterday's work, I hear someone whisper that he has left. He has walked through one of the gaps and out into the grey mist. No one who does such a thing ever returns. The mist is endless, just as the building is eternal and infinite. It is only we who build it who come to an end, die and have to be replaced. I raise my trowel, dripping with mortar: thick, heavy tears as grey as the fog. A careless action. Imperfect even to my eyes, this will be one of the first courses to be removed overnight but I cannot help myself. Now my mind is flooded with discontent. This life touches on being pointless. If in all my time the structure has increased by so little, what value has my contribution added to it? If my life is worthless, why continue with it?

I lay down my trowel, ignoring the growing chorus of confusion around me. No, I will not go on. Eternity bores me. This work bores me. My life bores me. I walk, then run, towards the gap in the wall. I call out to my friend to wait for me. If there is a path through the never thinning fog, I will take it. I will stride along it, brave until fear or death claim me.

Ahead the fog is shifting, clinging like long, damp fingers to my face and clothes as it splits, becoming thinner and thinner tendrils.

I glimpse my friend. I shout after him, "Wait! I want to come with you. I will walk beside you."

He turns and I see him frown at what he sees. He beckons to me and again I increase my pace. As I reach him he points behind me and whispers, "Look."

I join him and side by side we stare through the thinning grey.

This side of the wall there is another army of people, all intent on their work, their infinite, eternal work of removing the bricks and scraping away the layers of mortar from a wall that never stops growing but never gets any taller.

A TIME OF GREATEST NEED

"Good morrow, young squire. Where be the battle?"

The battle? I stared at the speaker, who had appeared from nowhere to block my path. He was nothing like the usual trespassers, with their backpacks and dogs. He was a young man, not much older than myself, wearing a suit of armour so well polished it reflected the early morning sun. He was leading a large, bay horse, also covered in shining, silver armour. He could have stepped out of a Pre-Raphaelite painting or even escaped from a theme park, but there was nothing like that anywhere close by. I had the fleeting thought I might be seeing a ghost. There were so many local tales associated with the Hill. I know I ought to have been scared but he was more comical than threatening. "I'm afraid there is no battle just now."

He mumbled something but his strange accent was so thick I had a little trouble making out the words. "Ah, so it's an invasion, is it? And I must be the first one of us to wake."

"You mean there are more of you?"

"Indeed. There are enough of us to take to the field and, although we did lose the last battle, we have had a long rest and are now ready for whatever comes. Tell me the worst. Who are the invaders we must face?"

"We're not being invaded by anyone. We're not at war."

His face fell. "Oh no! Please don't tell me the darkest hour is plague or pestilence. We'd be no use for that." He drew his sword from its scabbard and raised the weapon in front of his face. "My blade is sharp and true. I will wield it as I swore to do in the service of Albion. And my liege!"

"I'm not sure what King Charles would do with it. No one uses swords any more."

The weapon fell to his side, clanking against the metal of his armour. "No one uses swords? What kind of place is this, young squire?"

"I'm not a squire."

His eyes widened and he blushed. "You are a maiden?" He took a step back then bowed. "Forgive the error, fair lady. I do understand. You are fleeing. You have had to don your strange attire to hide your true self." Again he raised the blade. "I, Sir Lamorak, will be your champion. Show me your persecutor? I shall fight him for you."

"Er, no thanks. I'm not being persecuted at the moment and this is how lots of women dress nowadays."

There was a clanking from behind me. "Have you found the battle? Is the foe close by?" It was another man in fancy dress, wearing even more elaborate armour.

"No, Sir Geraint, this maiden says there's no one here to fight."

"There must be. This is the hour of greatest need, isn't it? Otherwise, why would we be here?"

They both looked at me.

I was becoming annoyed. "I think this joke has gone on long enough. There is no battle, no invasion; no trouble at all. You should go back to where you came from and stop being so silly."

The newcomer shook his head. "We can't go back. We're awake now. We've been asleep long enough."

"Where were you sleeping?" I hadn't noticed any tents on my way across the field.

"In that cave." Sir Lamorak pointed up the side of the hill.

I couldn't see any cave. There was nothing except a circular depression half way up filled with long grass.

With a low cry, he abandoned his horse and ran past me. In seconds he was standing in the centre of the depression. "Here! It was here. Oh, what has happened? What foul magic is this? Where is the king?"

Sir Geraint raced up to join him and, drawing their swords, they began stabbing at the tufts of grass, their blades sinking hilt deep in the damp ground. They pulled up clods of earth and threw aside the few stones, all the time becoming more and more frantic.

Sir Geraint shouted out a string of names, only one of which I recognised. "Oh, Lancelot, where are you?" He sank to his knees. "We have lost them, lost our comrades, lost our king! What are we to do?" He was close to tears.

Lamorak became still. He wiped his stained sword on some moss. "You know, we may have got this wrong. Perhaps the cave cannot be found because Merlin has hidden it. We might have been awoken to pursue a special quest. We were never told we would all wake together. Maybe this is a task for us and us alone."

They descended the slope and Lamorak sheathed his sword. "What do you think, maiden? Is there some small task Merlin might have brought us here to perform?"

I wanted to laugh at his earnest expression. "Merlin? I don't believe he ever existed. But if he did and King Arthur were asleep, it wouldn't be here. You're not even in the right country. The legends say he sleeps on the Isle of Avalon or somewhere in Wales, not under a little hill in East Anglia."

"Where's Wales? I've never heard of it. Have you, Geraint?"

The other man shook his head. "No, I haven't, nor any of those other places. We are in Albion."

"No, you're in England. It's 2024 and King Charles III is on the throne. Not Arthur. In any case, kings don't rule any more; we have a government now, not that they're any good at it. But you know all that. Let's stop this game, shall we?"

"What are you saying? The king has been deposed? That must be the reason we are here." Sir Geraint flourished his sword. "We shall begin our service to our royal master at once. Take us to him. Or is he in exile?"

"No, I think he's probably at Buckingham Palace. But I can't take you there. They'd never let us in."

"Ah, poor, unfortunate king, held prisoner in his own palace. Lamorak and I shall help to raise the siege."

This was too much. I wasn't sure what to do with them, especially as they were now brandishing their swords as though about to attack anything in reach. I was afraid someone might get hurt.

"Look, gentlemen, I've got an idea. Let's go to the farmhouse and you can tell my uncle your story; he loves anything like this."

"We have no time to visit with farmers. We must away to the capital and the king."

"Wait, Geraint. Maiden, if you will take us to the local lord, the owner of these lands, we would be prepared to visit with him."

"That would be my uncle. We're on part of his farm; at least it's his for now."

The two knights and their horses fell into step behind me but only after fretting about my taking the lead. They thought I might require their protection from any brigands, cutpurses or wolves we might encounter on the way.

We arrived at the farm to find my Aunt Philomena standing in the lane. "Oh, Sandra, am I glad you're here? Your Uncle Jonathan has got this strange..." She broke off as my two companions both bowed to her. "More of you, eh? What is going on? You'd better go in." She took the halters of both horses then stepped aside to let us enter.

My uncle was in the kitchen and with him was another stranger, also wearing armour.

Lamorak stepped forward. "Sir Bedivere, are you here too?"

"Indeed I am, my brothers. Allow me to present Lord Jonathan of Coates Farm."

"I've told you. I'm just Jonathan." My uncle gave a weary shrug.

"Lord Jonathan, are you the one who is to lead us until the king awakes?"

My uncle shook his head at Lamorak. "I wouldn't like to try. I don't even know why you're here. I'm not aware of any crisis bad enough to wake you up."

I was amazed. My uncle sounded as though he believed the wild story Lamorak and his friends were telling. Was it possible it could be true? "You think these men really are knights of the Round Table?"

"I didn't at first but, having listened to Bedivere and taken a good look at his horse and armour, I can't think of any other explanation."

"But surely the idea of a sleeping king with a cave full of knights is only a myth. And even if it weren't, why would they come here?"

"Well, there is one possibility. Perhaps we are the ones they have come to help." My uncle sat down on the nearest chair. "Remember the story your grandfather used to tell, the one where he said our family was descended from King Arthur. He had the tale from his own father, who always insisted it was true. What if it was?"

"It couldn't be. It was just a story."

"Maybe, but you know as well as I do the farm has never been in so much trouble. And these guys have come here the very day I've given up hope."

"Oh, please! As if they could help us save the farm. You know it can't be done."

Lamorak drew his sword again. "Maiden, what is the trouble of which you speak?"

"Nothing a sword can solve." My uncle sighed. "The business has been losing too much money recently. It can no longer be run at a profit. I'm having to sell up. I've even found a buyer; a company that wants to build luxury houses on this site. Look, I'll show you the plans." He picked up a large map from the dresser and unrolled it over the kitchen table.

The three knights exchanged glances. They shook their heads, no doubt disappointed there would be no fight for them to win. Or maybe they had never seen a map before.

It was the first time I had been shown what the builders intended to do and I was shocked at the extent of the proposed development; so many fields to be swallowed up and... My mouth fell open. "The Hill! Don't you see? It's the only one for miles around and they're going to flatten it."

Sir Lamorak paled. "But the king sleeps within the cave. If the Hill is destroyed..." He turned to his companions. "This is it, the reason we are awake. It is not Albion's hour of greatest need; it is our own. King Arthur must be saved! The Hill, our resting place, cannot be disturbed.

"It's worse than that."

Everyone looked at Bedivere.

He took a deep breath. "Our king and our fellow knights of the Round Table are not the only ones who rest here." He waved his hand at the land beyond the window. "This was the site of the Last Battle. Merlin took those of us he had chosen to accompany Arthur and placed us in the cave, but all around he left the bodies of those who had died. Many brave knights were slain that day. We protested to the wizard it was wrong to leave their bodies to the crows and the human scavengers who would come in their wake, so he granted us two days to give Christian rites and make a funeral pyre for as many as we could. We placed everything of value in a deep hole in the centre of the battlefield, then covered it over with soil and a large stone. We hoped it would be safe there until our awakening."

"I know what we did," Lamorak interrupted him. "But I don't see how it helps us defend the Hill. We can only wear one suit of armour and use one sword at a time. Having a dozen more won't make us better fighters."

"We're not going to fight." Bedivere laid his sword on the table. "I don't think Lord Jonathan requires fighters. What he needs is gold. Am I right, my lord?"

He nodded. "Not gold as such but certainly money. And a sword of this age in this condition would be worth a small fortune. How many do you think you placed in this hole on the battlefield?"

Bedivere scratched his chin. "We didn't count, but we know more than one hundred nobles and knights perished. And it's not only swords; there were breastplates, shields and some jewellery: rings and so on. Oh, and several bags of coin."

"Could you find the place where you buried it?"

"Of course, Lord Jonathan. What use would it have been if we had forgotten that? It was three hundred paces east of the entrance to the cave."

My uncle went to his study and fetched his compass. We all went to the barn for spades. Then the three knights led us back to the Hill.

There was the small problem of the cave having vanished, so we decided the best we could do was to take the centre of the depression as its probable location.

My uncle held up the compass and explained its use. I think only Bedivere understood and it was he who began pacing away from us.

Three hundred strides and there at our feet was a large, flat stone half hidden by moss.

Bedivere used the flat of his dagger to scratch the green away and in the centre was the impression of a cross. "Yes! Here it is. I carved this myself, Lord Jonathan."

It took all of us to lift the boulder out of the way. My heart was thumping. I had never been so excited. Uncle Jonathan was flushed and breathing hard, but the knights were quiet.

Geraint put down his spade. "We should not disturb this ground. The remains of our fallen comrades lie here."

Bedivere placed a hand on his shoulder. "Better we turn the earth than some stranger. And if we do not do this, what will become of our king? How will he sleep if the Hill is destroyed? Let Lord Jonathan take what lies beneath. Let him use it to preserve this place." He looked to my uncle. "That is what you will do, is it not? You will stop them destroying the Hill."

"I give you my word. If what we find here is enough to save the farm, I won't let anyone touch your Hill."

We dug until it was too dark to see but found nothing except fragments of flint and small stones. We agreed to give it a few more hours in the morning.

The next day was the last before my uncle would have to sign the contract allowing the builders to move in. I think he had already given up all hope. If Bedivere was wrong and there was nothing to be found at the bottom of the ever deepening hole, we would not have enough time to search the many acres of the farm.

Noon arrived and we still had nothing to show but blisters. Our time was up.

I lifted my spade for the final time and there, in the dark mud, I spotted the glistening richness of gold...

Once the threat to King Arthur and his men had been removed, I expected the knights to return to their slumber. So did they.

But the cave did not reappear.

Days passed and it became clear there was to be no reunion with their sleeping king. They wandered around the farm, listless and moping. The knights had saved the land but lost themselves. What were they to do in a world so different from their own?

"I miss fighting. If only there were a tourney I could attend." As he spoke, Lamorak beheaded half a bush of my aunt's favourite roses. "Or just an afternoon of single combat." There went the lupins.

Meanwhile, the other two knights, with lances improvised from boughs lopped off the apple tree, were riding at each other over the churned up ground of the kitchen garden.

My aunt, watching them out of the window, was not pleased. "Those three should find something useful to do. There they go: making a spectacle of themselves again. They can be seen from the road. Only yesterday I had four separate groups knocking at the door, asking if we sold cream teas during the interval."

It was then it struck me. "Aunt Phil, that's just what we should do. People pay good money to be entertained. What if we get the knights to show off their skills; put on an authentic tournament?"

And that, my friends, is how all this began. Welcome to Coates Medieval Experience, the most historically accurate theme park in the country. Why don't you talk with those men standing over there: Bedivere, Lamorak and Geraint? Let them show you their armour; it is correct in every detail. Try your hand at fencing. You won't stand a chance against them; for they are three of the original knights from King Arthur's Round Table!

I know it's hard to believe but it's all true.

Their comrades sleep on under the Hill. So tread softly as you take the tour; for if the sleeping king awakens, it will indeed be the hour of our greatest need.

A BASKET OF PEONIES

Under the watchful eyes of the two guards I shuffled into the dungeon. The brown haired one rushed past me and pulled out a heavy chair from beside the polished oak table. You would have thought me a fine lady, a guest of the house; not a prisoner.

"My lord has sent you a peach today. They're rare this time of year."

I was tempted to suggest if he liked peaches so much, he should eat it himself. Delicacies were no doubt a rarity on his pay. But he would have shrunk away if I had held it out to him. It was tainted fruit and all three of us knew it. The skin was soft and the flesh would have been tender but there was a tiny hole. A drop of juice glistened beside it. What had they put into it this time? Something to make me sick again? Or something worse? The tampering was not meant to be a secret. It was an invitation.

I could set the peach down again, refuse to obey his lordship's implied command, but they were watching me, waiting to see if I would perform. If I could perform.

I pretended to concentrate.

The guard leaned closer. It was a waste of time: there was nothing for him to learn.

"It's an apple, isn't it?"

He nodded. Why does the use of magic fascinate people so?

Holding up the fruit on the palm of my hand, I mimed a pair of scales. "Switch!"

The peach was gone and in its place was a small, crisp, green apple. I could smell the sweetness. My stomach rumbled, my mouth watered: I had not eaten in three days.

This time I had kept them waiting but in the end given them what they wanted. But only because it suited me. I had been a good girl, performed my little trick over a longer distance than the day before.

They let me keep the apple. It was my reward and they were not about to starve me. I wouldn't be of any use dead.

The two guards escorted me back to my tiny cell. The door closed behind them and I was locked in yet again.

Once sure they had finished with me for the day, I added the apple to the small collection of objects tied up in a scrap of cloth torn from the filthy bedsheet.

Time for a little concentration. Weighing the bundle in my hands and reaching out, I sensed something at the extreme edge of my range: a dish perhaps? Not sure and not wanting to know what it was, I pulled back. If I were not careful, that item would be in my hand instead of the object I needed.

My means of escape still eluded me. When the guards had first imprisoned me I caught a glimpse of the keys: three big, old pieces of dull metal clinking together on a large, iron ring. If I were holding something close to the same weight, I would be able to get those keys and get out of this place, but so far the meagre scraps accumulated in my bundle were nothing like enough.

How long had I been a prisoner? Keeping track of the days had proved impossible.

Perching on the edge of the hard bunk, I thought back to how I had got myself into this mess.

It all began with a dare. Many of the villagers said the old woman who lived on the corner near the smithy was a witch. I didn't believe she was and neither did anyone I knew but the finger had been pointed and you don't stand up for anyone once that happens. In any case she wasn't one of us. She was from the country over the mountains and there were rumours about that place. It was said there was a witch in every street.

The old woman was tried and found guilty. No one expected any other verdict. A pyre was constructed in the village square and three men were sent to fetch her. But she was no longer there; her cell was empty.

The cottage she lived in had been left abandoned. No one was brave enough to set foot inside. Until, months later, on the night of Halloween, my friends and I dared each other to enter.

It was late. An owl hooted as we five girls huddled together on the front step and Maud, the eldest of us, pushed open the door. It was Annie who found the old, metal bound box. There was nothing else in the cottage except a few broken plates and some rickety, old furniture.

We gathered round Annie.

Maud nudged her. "Why don't you open it?"

I was a little afraid but we all agreed there must be something valuable in the box, maybe a few coins or some jewels.

The lid splintered into a thousand pieces as Annie raised it. Inside was an old, yellowed parchment. A single word was written on it. I felt as if it was calling out to me. My fingers itched to touch it. Besides, what use would it have been to any of the others? I was the only one of us who had learned to read.

I snatched it from Annie's hand.

The parchment was warm to the touch. The single word was "Switch". As I unfolded the document more words appeared. They blazed like tiny fires. I began shouting in some strange language. My mouth started to bleed, blisters sprang up on my tongue and my throat was full of razors yet I could not stop reading. As I came to the end of the words, smoke curled around my fingers and, with a loud sizzle, the paper disintegrated, descending to the ground at my feet in a shower of red hot ashes.

From that moment on I was infected with witchcraft. If I held an object and thought of something similar, not always but often the objects changed places. I soon discovered the size and shape made no difference but if the weights were close enough, the spell (for I had decided it must be a spell) would exchange the items for each other.

At first I didn't see what use this could be to me or anyone else but soon realised all that was required was a pebble of similar weight and I could swap it for a coin in someone else's pocket. In no time I became adept at judging weights with some accuracy. So I gave in to temptation and became a thief.

It took a while for the thefts to be linked to me but once they were, I had to leave the village in a hurry. Up to that point the switches had only been small objects but, in order to get away, I had to try for something bigger: something living.

Running to the back of the nearby stables, I found a large rock, placed my hand on it and closed my eyes.

"Switch!"

I didn't really believe it could work but my fingers tangled in the mane of the finest horse in the village, sixteen hands of grey perfection. It took me a little longer to find the next boulder of the right weight.

"Switch!"

The saddle was not of the best quality but not the worst either. I rode away into the gathering twilight.

In the next village...

"Switch!"

And I discovered a new, crisp loaf of bread from the bakers weighed no more or less than a couple of shirts stolen from a washing line. For a while it was all such great fun.

"Switch!" A juicy ham in exchange for an old, wooden bucket found beside a doorstep.

"Switch!" A pat of creamy, yellow butter in exchange for a handful of dried up leaves.

"Switch!" A knife to cut the meat in exchange for a small branch fallen by the side of the road.

"Switch!" A cup of milk in exchange for a broken jug.

Breakfast over, I continued on my journey without a single concern about the trail of confusion left behind in my wake.

The next night, having used the spell a few more times, there was money enough for a soft bed in a warm inn. But on undressing I found my left boot was stuck. My toes would not bend. They wouldn't move at all. I couldn't even wriggle them. This was worrying. Was something broken? No, because if it was, wouldn't I be in pain?

At last I managed to tug the boot free. Inside the stocking something was amiss. Staring at my foot, I saw the little toe and the one next to it were no longer flesh and blood. Instead they were the colour and texture of granite. I stifled a scream. I was turning to stone! It could only be as a result of using the spell.

This had to stop before I caused any more harm to myself and, what was even more important, I must find the old witch and persuade her to repair the damage and take back her spell.

I soon discovered giving up was not as easy as I had thought it would be. All the money I had switched for pebbles had gone and travel was impossible without the means to buy food. Worse, within the day came another discovery. The power of the spell and the temptation to use it were both getting stronger. Whenever I placed my hand on an object, anything nearby of a similar weight became visible to me, like a faint overlay on top.

I reached the next town but on the way...

"Switch!"

I couldn't help myself. The hunger pangs were too bad so a pile of earth was exchanged for a pork pie cooling on the windowsill of a farmhouse. At least I was spared feeding the horse as there was plenty of grass around us for him to eat.

My circumstances left me with no choice other than to continue to use the power.

"Switch!" More stones were exchanged for another pocketful of coins in order to buy supplies for my journey to the mountains and the border beyond.

That night I discovered another of my toes, this time on my right foot, had turned to stone. The petrification of my body was speeding up.

I should have reached the mountain pass which led into the witch's country only two days later but the horse threw a shoe. Tired and not thinking, before realising what I had done...

"Switch!" The new horse might have weighed the same but he was a different animal altogether, a proud stallion without a saddle. He eyed me, tossing his head. I thought he might be challenging me to climb on his back.

A shout rang out from behind me. "Stand still, witch. We've got you surrounded." A group of five or six men brandishing swords emerged from the undergrowth.

Unable to flee, I threw up my hands and remained beside the horse.

The first one to reach me grabbed me by both arms and wrenched them round my back, while another produced a grubby piece of cloth and gagged me, hissing into my face, "There you are, witch. Try and harm us now." He picked me up and, after tying my legs together, tossed me across the horse. "Lord Farley wants to meet you."

They took me to a castle. At first my captor introduced himself with an apology. I was a lady of power and he respected my kind. He was charming. We ate together but I drank a little too much wine and made the mistake of believing him when he said he didn't intend to harm me. I told him the truth and showed him my feet. By that stage all of my toes had turned to stone.

I woke in a cell. Lord Farley explained his neighbour had something he would like to have: a large jewel. If I were to steal it for him, he would allow me to continue on my way. It would be easy. After all, it was not as if there was any need for me to break into his neighbour's well guarded stronghold. I could get close with a worthless object of a suitable size and simply switch them over.

We both knew he had no intention of releasing me. I was too useful. There would always be other neighbours, other objects.

I told him the spell would only work close to the target. He began testing me to determine my limits. I began biding my time until I had enough material to equal the weight of the dungeon keys. I intended to make my escape while it was still possible.

Still sitting on the bunk and grasping my bundle tight in my hand, I wondered how much more stuff would be needed to make the switch happen. I wouldn't be able to even envisage the keys until the weights were close to a perfect match.

A sound from the doorway: the key turning in the lock. It had to be the middle of the night. Couldn't his lordship sleep?

A guard I had never seen before blocked the light of the guttering torches in the corridor. He pushed the door closed behind him. The look on his face made me shiver.

"I never 'ad a witch."

I cowered away from him. "I'm not a witch. Leave me alone."

"Why should I?" Hot breath stinking of beer struck my face as he leant over my bunk. "Lord Farley won't protect ya. 'E wants results. Told 'im I could get 'em for 'im." His heavy sword belt clattered onto the stone floor.

There was nowhere to run.

Coarse fingers grasped my chin. "Don't worry, sweetie. Ya might even enjoy it."

Still clasping the bundle to my chest, I suddenly felt something of equal weight crying out to me.

"Switch!"

He fell in slow motion as his heart, now in my hand, beat one final time.

Casting the sticky, bleeding mess into the far corner, I struggled to my feet and bent over the dead body to take his dagger. On touching the hilt I sensed the locations of several others so I knew where all the guards were.

Beyond the door no one was in sight. The corridor was empty. I doubted my would be assailant had obtained his master's permission to assault me: it was more likely he had persuaded his fellow guards to make themselves scarce, which was good for me.

My progress along the passage was slow, as I was unable to run with all but the heels of both feet made of stone. The weight was manageable but it was impossible to bend or flex them, which made climbing the stairs torture. When at last I gained the landing my ears were filled with music wafting down from the floor above. His lordship must have been holding a ball or something, which would explain how the guard had managed to sneak down to my cell.

Two daggers were not far away but neither was on the path I was taking. Reaching the ground floor of the castle, I picked up the feel of other objects along a side corridor: not daggers but knives, pots, a wooden board, all of them the exact weight of the object in my hand but not one of them worth switching for.

On reaching the kitchen, everyone in sight was busy. No one noticed me or, if they did, they didn't raise the alarm.

Outside at last, free of the confines of the castle dungeons, breathing in the cool night air and with a full moon and thousands of stars glimmering above me, I wanted to shout for joy but it was too soon. My escape was not yet complete. Even so, I took the time to stoop down and wash my sticky fingers in the water of a large pond at the side of the drive.

There was no need to find the stables. Several horses were tied to a rail at the front of the building. A couple of men, no doubt supposed to be keeping an eye on the mounts, were sitting with their backs to me on a low wall. I untethered a horse from the far end of the line and, holding my breath, led the animal away in silence.

Once through the main gate I mounted my stolen steed and we cantered away.

Two days after my escape, hopeful of finding my witch without further delay, I at last reached the far side of the mountains. It was unfortunate there had been no way to avoid the occasional switch. Both of my ankles were now lost to the encroaching petrification and my legs ached when I walked. I was becoming more and more afraid.

A small village slumbered on the slopes leading down from the pass. I took water from the well in the square and let the horse drink from the trough next to it. We were both hungry but what kind of food was worth my left calf?

Looking around me, some of the houses had metal or wooden objects swinging from their eaves. They were both familiar and strange at the same time. In my own village there were signs something like these. The baker had a wooden loaf, the shoemaker a metal boot and the smith an oversized horseshoe. In this village I saw a rain cloud made from dull metal from which descended a shining, flashing bolt of lightning. Next door was a rope which uncoiled itself, reached the ground and vanished, only to reappear and repeat the pattern. Another house had ears of corn which changed from tender shoots to a golden sheaf and back again.

I had found the witches! But which witch was mine? There was no sign displaying someone turning to stone.

A young girl skipped across the square. Something was odd about her. Her hair was changing colour from one moment to the next.

She approached me. "What are you staring at?"

"Why, your hair... It's so unusual."

"Oh, don't you start. I have to live with this until it fades away. My mother says it serves me right for stealing someone else's spell." She looked me up and down. "You've come from over the mountains, haven't you?"

"Yes, I have."

"So what are you after? Weather spells? That's what most people come here for." She waved at the house with the thundercloud. "That's where you should go. Mrs. Knowles writes the best ones."

"No, it's not a weather spell." Slumping down against the wall of the well, I showed her my feet. "I have to find help for these."

She shook her head. "You've been using someone else's magic as well, haven't you? Stealing spells when you have no powers of your own will always land you in trouble."

"What can I do about it?"

"Depends who you stole the spell from."

I described the old woman.

The girl wrinkled her nose. "You should have chosen someone else to annoy. She won't let you off without it costing you. I wouldn't like to be in your shoes." She giggled. "Not that you need them any more!"

"Where do I find this woman?"

"Not here. She lives in the next town. You follow the main road for a day and a half. When you get there, ask for Lady Moira."

I picked up the reins of my horse. "Thank you."

"Oh, that's all right. There is one thing, though. Don't try using that stolen spell this side of the mountains. It will have ten times the effect. You'd be stone from head to toe before you knew it."

Trembling at the thought of it, I thanked her again and followed the road. Despite my rumbling stomach, no switch spell was used that day.

I spent the night in the open, sleeping beside the horse, cold and uneasy, and woke damp from the dew, shivering. An inn was close by. Overcome by the aroma of frying bacon, I was so tempted to switch some of the pebbles on the path for a morsel of food or a warm drink.

Just before noon I reached my destination: the main street of the next town. As in every other settlement in the area there was a fountain so at least I didn't go thirsty.

I asked a man filling a large jug if he knew where to find Lady Moira.

Straightening his back, he gave me an odd look. "Are you sure you want to find her? Whatever the problem, you'd do better turning back. She never helps anyone except herself."

"I have to see her. There's something of hers I must return."

"Oh well, you have been warned." He pointed to a large house at the far end of the street.

As the horse approached the gates, they flung themselves aside. I was expected. Dismounting, I started up the path.

Before I could reach the door, it too opened by itself. A beautiful, young woman about my age, not an ugly old crone, stood on the threshold. She had hair the colour of ripe grain, which changed as I watched to a deep red. There was no doubt this was the girl from the square.

"You tricked me. I had already found you."

"You had but I wanted to punish you a little more. You shouldn't have stolen my spell."

"I'm sorry. I didn't intend to steal it and now all I want to do is give it back."

"Then why don't you?"

"How do I do that?"

"Like this." She took my arm and led me into her garden.

I had never seen so many different flowers in one place. Some of them were not even in season. We stood by a pond covered in water lilies and surrounded by a profusion of multicoloured roses.

"Here we are. Now cup your hands together. That's it. Just right."

"What do I do now?"

"To give the spell back you must tell it to finish with you. There's nothing else you need to do. Just say, 'Switch, finish!'."

I took a deep breath and spoke the words, "Switch, finish!"

They were my last.

You see, witches are tricky and the words they use in their spells can have more than one meaning. The ending of the spell was also the ending of me.

Here I stand in the witch's garden. She has placed a basket of peonies in my hands. When they fade she will replace them. She says, of all her statues I am her favourite.

She wouldn't switch me for anything.

ART

With a beaming smile she ushers us inside. "Welcome to our lovely, new re-education centre: six floors dedicated to your every need. You'll never want to set foot outside again."

I don't think I've ever met a worse salesperson in my entire life. I can't think of a single reason to believe anything she says, not to mention she has succeeded in misjudging every one of the fifteen people in this room.

Take that one over by the wall: the guy with the shock of bleached blond hair and the over-developed muscles; he's trying hard not to make it obvious but he's looking for the way out, and we've only just arrived! I think maybe I'll join him soon. I don't much care for the feel of this place.

"Excuse me, miss?" Silly girl, putting her hand up. Does she think she's still at school? Mind you, she is rather young. She can't be much more than sixteen.

"I'm sorry, Emily, I don't have time to answer any questions just now. I'm only here to give you a general overview of what to expect. Your Individual Guidance Operative will be able to help you with any personal issues you may have." Oh, I so hate corporate smiles and this woman has the best example of one I've ever seen.

Poor Emily bites her lip. I'm pretty sure she won't be asking anything else for a while.

"Where's the dining room? No one's even offered us so much as a cup of coffee yet."

Corporate smile beams at corpulent man in crumpled lounge suit. "Tell me, sir, are you thirsty? Is your stomach rumbling?"

"Well no, but a cup of coffee is the very least any visitor would expect in a place like this, isn't it?"

"No, it isn't and we don't have any. Come along now, everybody. As I said, all your needs will be met in due course. Now, we are about to proceed to the next floor. We have a lot to get through this morning."

"No coffee? What sort of organisation is this?" the corpulent man grumbles to himself under his breath as we follow our guide as she leads us up a long, curving staircase. It reminds me of the ones you see in those old Fred Astaire dance movies from the nineteen thirties.

"Don't you have a lift?"

"No, madam, we have stairs instead. They were invented first, you know." Though our guide's tone has now become sarcastic, her corporate smile doesn't waver.

The room at the top of the stairs is like nowhere I have been before. The thick pile carpet is off white and it's like your feet are sinking into something between a meringue and a blancmange.

We tiptoe over to a set of tall windows; some arched, some square, some round but not one of them has curtains or blinds. Now, this is odd. They can't be windows after all. They must be some sort of clever art work because each one looks out on a different vista. On the left is what can only be a panorama over the Grand Canyon at sunset, whilst to my right is a view of Sydney Harbour Bridge in the early morning.

A tall, thin woman walks over to it, presses her forehead to the glass and places her arms on the wide sill. "Can I stay here for a while, please?"

"If you wish. I'll send someone to collect you if you get bored."

"Oh, I won't get bored."

Our guide gives the woman's shoulder a gentle squeeze. "No, dear, I don't think you will." She makes a mark on a thin pad of paper I hadn't noticed she was carrying until now.

Our party is reduced to twelve by the time we leave the room with the windows.

Muscleman and a girl in a leotard who is chewing gum gasp in simultaneous delight as the next door is thrown open to reveal a huge gym cluttered with a dizzying array of uncomfortable static bikes, cross-trainers and machines with heavy weights attached. Oblivious of the rest of us, leotard girl races over to the nearest treadmill.

Nine of us trail behind our hostess up to the next floor.

I'm struggling to remember how I came to be here. It's as though my mind is filled with a kind of fog. I wonder if I've been drugged. I'm thinking this is some elaborate scheme to get me to talk about the new process. If it is, they're taking their time. No one has asked me a single question yet. Anyway, they'll be wasting their energy if they do. I have a nice promotion waiting for me when the new plant goes live. I'm not about to put that on the line. I've never wanted anything so much in my life and, well, I've certainly earned it.

I've not been paying attention. We're in another room now. The corpulent man is still annoying our hostess by telling her how to do her job. He's on about refreshments again but he's not fooling me. Or her for that matter. The drink he wants isn't coffee. It's something quite a lot stronger: whisky or brandy maybe.

Well, well, well. Who'd have guessed there'd be an old fashioned pub tucked away in one of the rooms beyond the gym? Plush sofas and easy chairs, a bar complete with pumps of real ale and a shelf groaning with vintage whiskies.

We leave three of our shrinking group sitting together at a table. They each raise a glass to us as the door closes on them.

I've had enough. It is time I got out of here, time to slip away while everyone's attention is distracted by the aquarium stretching out around the walls of the next room. I hear one of the men say he's an expert on corals and he's never seen so many rare examples in one place.

As I re-enter the bar, Emily follows me. "Can I come with you? I have to get home."

"Why not? The more the merrier," I reply though it's the opposite of what I'm thinking. One alone might get out of this place without attracting attention. But two? I'm becoming more and more convinced I have been kidnapped and this is some strange, elaborate cage.

Emily and I reach the staircase. We're in luck. It's crowded. At least fifty people are pushing their way up. I can't see who is in charge of them. Maybe their guide is in the centre of the crowd, trying to deal with all the complaints: "My luggage, where's my luggage?" and "I'm going to be late for a very important appointment" are among the comments drifting past us as we crush through the centre of the pack.

We've returned to the room where we first started. It's deserted.

Emily rushes towards the main doors. "I have to get home. I want to see my mother." She fumbles with the handle. "I have to tell her she was right about Robert all along."

"Why? What did she say about him?" I don't really want to know but it's polite to ask.

"She said he would hurt me. And look." She pulls aside her long, brown hair and I'm looking at a vivid red scar across the base of her neck. "Last night he tried to strangle me and I passed out. He must have abandoned me there because he was gone when I came round."

Despite the warmth in the room, I shiver. She is right. She ought to go home to her mother.

Outside on the street we say our goodbyes. She doesn't have far to go. As it happens we are close to where her parents live.

I think about taking a taxi but it's not far to the office either. I decide to walk and to enjoy the sun on my back.

No one acknowledges me from the reception desk. Janet doesn't even look up as I pass her.

My office door is open. Hargreaves is sitting in my chair. He has all my working papers on the process spread out in front of him. He's muttering my name and he's not sounding at all happy. No wonder. The process is my invention. I'm careful; I keep a clear desk and write sensitive information in a code of my own devising. This will be my personal legacy. No corporate spy will ever take anything away from me.

I lean forward over the desk. "What do you think you're doing, Hargreaves? From the way you're behaving, anyone would assume you thought I was dead. How pathetic! You have no ideas of your own so you try to steal mine."

He doesn't react. He picks up a single sheet of paper and holds it up to the light, as though he thinks it will help him.

"Ahem." A quiet cough from behind me.

I turn.

A young man is leaning on the door frame.

"Who are you? What do you want?"

"I want you. It's time to go back to the Centre. My name is Art, not that it matters. All you need to know is I'm your IGO, your individual guidance operative. Shall we be on our way?"

As he takes me by the hand, swan-like wings fan out from his broad shoulders to envelop me.

HOW TO MURDER A GHOST

I never knew it was possible for a ghost to be as afraid as I am right now.

A shiver passes through me. The words which will end me are being uttered. I can't escape. There is nowhere to go. The man in the chapel, ringing his little bell, waving his book by the light of a guttering candle means me no harm. He wants to free a trapped soul. He believes I am in torment but he is wrong. I don't want to cease to exist but I am already fading. I should never have come to...

"...Ackland Hall, ladies and gentlemen, the country seat of Lord and Lady Ackland, reputed to have no less than seven ghosts in residence: one of the most haunted sites in the country, which..."

I tuned out the tour guide's monotonous voice. He had no idea what he was talking about. This house might once have been as he described it but not any longer. It was almost deserted. No, not by the tourists. They come by the coachload to sit in the cafe and eat the scones cooked to "the original Victorian recipe created by Mrs. Grey, the original Victorian cook". Yeah, right. She nipped down to Sainsbury's for them too, did she?

In fact I was the only ghost in the house. Three never existed in the first place, being the inventions of guides over the years, and the remaining three have all been murdered in cold blood by the man in the chapel wielding bell, book and candle.

Yes, I was the last, except... I shouldn't have been there at all. I had answered an advert in Ghosts Abroad. It's an interesting publication. I've consulted it a few times. It lists haunt swaps available throughout the U.K. and Western Europe. The principle is simple. If you get bored with the place where you met your end, you exchange, for a limited period, with another spectre who is just as bored. We spirits have discovered by trial and error that, so long as both the ghosts are agreeable and swap places at the same time, there is no problem. However, you can't go to a place which has no resident ghost and you can't increase the number of ghosts in any location except by more untimely deaths. It's a bit restrictive but it does work.

So, let me tell you about the advert. It had been placed by Lady Josephine Ackland. A spoilt, jilted debutante, she died by hurling herself off the mock battlements of her family's country estate. In the advert she listed the advantages of her place: lovely views, paintings to wobble, pottery to jiggle, draughts available in all main rooms; the perfect haunt for a summer holiday. All I had to offer in exchange was a first floor bedsit with an old, faulty heating system prone to giving off noxious fumes. No dramatic death for me, I'm sorry to say.

I was surprised when she replied to my enquiry at once. She explained that after two hundred plus years of luxury she fancied slumming it for a month or two.

Swap arranged, I told my best friend Sam about it. He was a chimney sweep when the tenement building was a bit grander. He got stuck and starved to death.

He pulled a face, dislodging a few flakes of soot onto the bedsit carpet. I like it when he does that. It confuses the hell out of the current occupant. "There's something odd about Ackland Hall. I saw it in Dead News a few months ago."

"Well, what was it?"

"Can't remember but I think it was about a swap being cancelled at the last minute because the ghost at the hall had suddenly become unavailable for some reason."

I didn't listen. I never do. I was dreaming of drifting round corridors in a long, white dress and standing on the battlements with the wind in my tresses. Lady Josephine had promised me the use of her wardrobe. She was a generous host. Or so I thought.

Our swap took place at midnight. They all do and I saw Josephine in passing.

She called out to me, "Sorry about this. Try not to be too upset. It's nothing personal."

I shouted back, "Have a good time. See you in a month."

I arrived at the point from which she had departed. The battlements were rather high. I looked down over the edge but it was too dark and I couldn't see much. I wasn't afraid of falling. A ghost can't be hurt that way. Chances are I would have drifted down as though I were wearing a parachute but I wasn't about to try it. What I did want was to locate Josephine's wardrobe and get into some more appropriate gear. Who ever heard of an eighteenth century miss wearing Levis?

As I made my way down the grand, central staircase a young girl in a maid's uniform appeared at the bottom.

Her mouth fell open as she caught sight of me. "She did it, didn't she?"

"Hello, I'm Claudia. I'm haunt swapping with..."

"...Lady Josephine. I know but you must go back. You can't stay here. It's..."

She flickered. I can't think of any other way to describe it. She flickered again, becoming ever more transparent, like a breeze blowing through mist.

"Josephine tricked you. There's a... an exorcist..." On the last, terrifying word she gave a howl and was gone.

Shocked, I stared at the empty patch of air. I could hear a faint sound, not her but a chant. Josephine had provided a guide book along with the other paperwork involved in our exchange. I knew where each room was and I had no doubt the sound was coming from the old chapel.

I may not be the most courageous of ghosts but there was nothing for it. I had to find out what was happening.

I passed through the thick, oak door into what should have been an empty stone chamber, the pews and altar having been removed when the chapel was deconsecrated. The first thing I noticed was the acrid stench of sage. Pooh! The room was strewn with it and bunches of it were suspended either side of a space in the centre. A group of six people knelt there in a rough line in front of a tall, dark haired man. He stood behind a table draped in white linen on top of which were a small brass bell, a large book and a thin, white candle in a silver holder. He wore a thick, grey habit with a hood but I could still see the cuffs of his jeans and a pair of expensive trainers peeking out from the bottom of it.

"Go to your rest, Eliza!" He beamed at his audience. "It is done. There is now only Lady Josephine Ackland left for us to help on her way. We will reconvene tomorrow at midnight."

His audience scrambled to their feet and left the room, patting each other on the back.

He began packing his instruments of torture into a holdall. He stopped and looked at me. "I know you're here. I can't see you but I can sense your presence. I've been a medium since I was born. Tomorrow, I promise I will help you. I will release your unhappy spirit and send you to your eternal rest. Poor, trapped ghost, I will free you."

Poor, trapped ghost? I was, wasn't I? Josephine had conned me into taking her place. I was going to be murdered and there was nothing I could do about it. I would cease to exist.

The next morning I tried to contact Ghosts Abroad through the ether but it was the weekend and there was no one available to help me. I wouldn't be able to leave the building unless I found some other poor sucker to replace me and I wouldn't have done that even if I could.

I watched the tour party as they wandered round with their annoying guide. I had a half baked idea I might be able to find a psychic among them who could intercede. All I did manage to do was irritate a golden retriever who was busy guiding her blind mistress.

The party ate their scones and left.

It was five o'clock. In a couple of hours, though I did not want to go, I would be drawn to the battlements and have to stay there for a while. It was one of the conditions of the swap. Every day, at the time the event occurred, I had to walk up and down around the spot where Josephine plunged to her death. Would this be the last time anyone did this? With no ghost in residence, Josephine could not return.

Afterwards I drifted through the rooms. I hoped she felt guilty for what she was doing to me.

As midnight approached I went to the chapel. The man was already there, setting up his table and setting out new bunches of sage. Busy, busy.

I plucked at his sleeve but he didn't react. I blew into his face. Nothing happened. He wasn't as psychic as he thought he was. I couldn't get through to him at all. If he knew I was there, he gave no sign of it.

I left the room and went down to the entrance hall. As each of his friends arrived I tried everything I could think of to attract their attention. They shivered with delight as I, frantic with fear, stirred the curtains, chilled them with icy breath and threw pottery from shelves so it smashed at their feet. Only one of them spoke to me and she was facing the wrong direction at the time.

"Oh, sad little ghost, don't worry. Nick will soon release you from your torment."

There was nothing more I could do. My last hope was gone.

The exorcism has begun. I sensed it the exact moment the chanting started. I was in the drawing room, standing before a portrait of Josephine. I made it fall off the wall but I knew it wasn't damaged. Petty of me but it was all I could do.

Tomorrow the guide will tell his coach party it happened during the night and one of the seven ghosts was responsible. Some of them will go "Ooh!" and some "Ah!". Some will not believe. They will say there are no ghosts at Ackland Hall...

...and they will be right.

GOLDEN APPLE INC.

"What do you think?"

"I think your dog won."

He arched his eyebrows. "And yours lost?"

"Yes but only by a nose." I pinched my own to emphasize how small a margin it had been.

The steward stuck his head out of the booth. "Is there a problem, gentlemen? I hope your dogs are going to be the only combatants we have to pull apart this evening."

We both laughed. "No, not at all. It's Philo's win fair and square. This guy deserves the prize and Philo can take the cake."

Announcement made, Philo's owner invited me to help him spend his prize money by having a drink with him in the bar. A "consolation prize," he called it. We sat at a table overlooking the track.

"You don't know who I am, do you?"

"No. Once again you have the advantage. My name's Paris, Paris Priam." I put out my hand and he shook it. His grip would have put a wrestler to shame.

"Pleased to meet you, Paris. They call me Ares Theopoulos."

Ah, that explained why he looked familiar. He had to be the son of my employer, Zeus Theopoulos.

He gave out a throaty chuckle. "From your expression I'd say I've surprised you. You don't happen to work for the Corporation, do you?"

"Actually, I do. I'm the principal in charge of security here at the London office."

He clapped me on the back. "Well, it's good to know we have such an honest and fair man working for us. I'll be sure to mention you to my father."

Yeah, right. Old Zeus Theopoulos wasn't the best employer I'd ever had. He wasn't known for showing fairness towards his staff or even in dealings with his suppliers. He had a bad reputation with the ladies too.

After a long night and a lot of wine I returned to work with a sore head and assumed that would be the last time I would meet any of the Theopoulos family face to face. It has always been somewhat of a nepotistic operation. The family is large, mainly due to the patriarch having run through several girlfriends and casual flings. The old man would then insist on bringing many of the illegitimate children he had fathered into the family firm, in addition to his legitimate offspring with his long suffering wife.

A few months went by. Rumours began to circulate about problems on the board. An independent consultant, Ms. Eris, had sown discord by proposing the merger of two divisions, Thetis Chemicals and Peleus Pharmaceuticals, and the splitting off of a third, the Eastern Mediterranean operation, Golden Apple Inc. She advised the latter should be run by the "fairest" member of the family, whatever that was supposed to mean. It was a major subsidiary with revenues and profits into the millions.

Three contenders put their names forward: Zeus's wife, Hera, and two of his daughters, Athena and Aphrodite. There was no question of them sharing. They were known throughout the Corporation to have an intense dislike of one another. In my office the problem was referred to as "the beauty contest".

I didn't take much interest in it. What had it to do with me? Then out of the blue I received a phone call from Ares.

"How's that greyhound of yours doing, Paris?"

"Not bad. He keeps himself in food and kennel fees. He won a race only last week. I hear you sold Philo."

"Yeah, I got bored with the whole dog thing. I'm into horses now but that's not why I'm calling today; I've got a message for you from my pa."

"Oh?" This was strange. How had I come to the attention of the great Zeus Theopoulos?

"He was impressed by how sporting you were in admitting my dog won the race that day. He wants someone who shows good judgment to do a little job for him."

The luxury jet at last touched down between the golden sand dunes and the lush formal gardens of Olympus, the Theopoulos family's private island. Despite the opulence surrounding me, the politeness of the staff who greeted me and their exhortations to enjoy my stay, I was under no illusions as to the reason for my invitation: what the 'little job' might be.

Ares and his father both met me from the plane and right away confirmed my fears were well founded. I was to spend some time with each of the three ladies and it would be my decision which one would receive the prize. I could already taste the poison in the chalice. These were three powerful businesswomen and I was going to come out of this mess with at least two of them as my enemies.

The boss reassured me. As of tonight I was my own man. The small company my family owned, Ilium Industries, had just been given a huge order to supply ships to the Theopoulos empire. We would be wealthy. I could at last afford to leave the Corporation and go to work alongside my father, my older brother, Hector, and my sister, Cassie. Perhaps now she could stop being so pessimistic about the family's future, always predicting disasters which beggared belief.

Zeus thumped me on the arm and joked that I might found a dynasty as powerful as his own. All I needed was to find the right woman to marry.

Day one.

Hera Theopoulos came to pick me up from the main residence in her red Porsche. She drove at breakneck speed on a white knuckle ride round the many hairpin bends leading up to the top of the island's highest peak.

When I had stopped shaking I clambered out of the car to join her on the narrow viewing platform overlooking much of the island.

She swept her long arm across the fertile fields, the golden sands, the blue sea. "All this is mine, you know. Zeus gave it to me as a wedding present. I own quite a few other islands in the Aegean and several bits of Africa too." She batted her eyelids at me. "I would be so grateful if I were to be given control of Golden Apple. If you chose me, I wouldn't have any time to enjoy all this. I would be prepared to give it away."

"Are you trying to bribe me, Mrs. Theopoulos?"

"Why not? Look at what you would gain."

I looked. I saw. I was tempted. I would become a king in all but name... but I was not about to give her my answer there and then. I had an inkling her two rivals might have their own ideas as to what would be a suitable reward for my recommendation.

That evening Zeus held a party. The wine flowed and I discovered Ares was a rather accomplished drummer. As he performed with his friends a woman got up from her table to sing along with the band.

I stared at her. I could not take my eyes off her. She was the most beautiful creature I had ever seen.

"Who is that?" I asked the vice president for sales, whose table I had been assigned to.

"Oh, her name is Helen. Her mother is Leda Tyndareus, a close friend of the boss if you know what I mean." My informant's wink left no doubt as to what he was suggesting.

I spent the remainder of the party trying and failing to get myself introduced to the gorgeous Ms. Tyndareus.

Day two.

I couldn't get Helen out of my head. I wasn't in the mood for a day in the company of Athena Theopoulos. She was far too clever for me. All she could talk about was acquisitions, mergers and money. She took me by private speedboat over to the mainland and we toured a factory which manufactured parts for aeroplane engines. She was all commerce, all business, all corporate. I knew for certain Golden Apple would thrive with her at its helm.

Over lunch she let me in on her expansion plans... then she told me about mine.

"I will make you rich. My people have designed a supercomputer so sophisticated you will never make a bad business decision again. You will be a warrior in the boardroom and you will rise all the way to the top echelons of the Forbes list."

But all the time she was laying out the terms of her bribe I could think of nothing but Helen.

That evening, another party. More wine but I wasn't thirsty. My eyes were filled with the stunning vision which was Helen, that night dressed in a long, shimmering gown of swan's feathers. So lovely, so talented, when she danced it was as though she floated on air. I was entranced, but try as I might I still couldn't get near her.

Day three.

It was my last day on the island. Zeus expected my decision by nightfall.

Aphrodite did not come to me. Instead she sent her chauffeur with a summons to her secluded villa.

I found her sunbathing, naked except for a pair of Dolce and Gabbana sunglasses, beside a large, azure blue swimming pool.

She removed her shades and fixed me with her large, green eyes. She said only one word.

"Helen."

"I beg your pardon."

"Helen Tyndareus, my and Athena's unacknowledged half sister. She's under contract to me. She models my friend's swimwear line, 'Made by Menelaus'. If you like, I will reassign her contract to you. She could be the face to launch your family's new line in luxury yachts. Maybe she could be more than that. She told me she really likes you. She likes you a lot. Menny will be livid at losing her, of course, but I'm sure you won't let that put you off."

And so it has been settled. On my recommendation Zeus will give Golden Apple Inc. to Aphrodite, though I do wonder what it is going to cost me and my family in the long run... As I left with Helen on my arm, I caught sight of Athena whispering into Menelaus's ear. They broke off to glare at me.

I now realise this contest is not over. Perhaps it will not be over for a very long time.

HOW TO MEND A BROKEN WING

There was a daemon at the bottom of my garden. I'd have liked to invite him inside but he was much too hot and I didn't want to burn the house down. Not when there was so much mortgage still outstanding and I was way behind on my insurance payments.

He said to call him Blizzard (I would never have been able to pronounce his name) and he wasn't a very important daemon, in fact quite a minor denizen of Hell. He had never got any further than the outermost circle.

When I found him he was in a bad way. Two of his wings had been slashed to ribbons and his skin was lacerated with deep gashes, from which liquid fire trickled onto the parched ground.

The day before, there had been a lawn where he was lying, but around two o'clock he and another of his kind had crashed through the high wall separating my little place from the sprawling grounds of the stately home next door. They were in the centre of a huge fireball: two indistinct shapes writhing within the conflagration, locked in a deadly battle, the larger one tearing the smaller apart. The flames were an unnatural spectrum of colours: white with flares of blood red and flashes reaching into the sky like jet black rockets, trailing purple smoke bearing all the hues of old bruises.

The fight did not last long. It was too uneven a contest. The air was filled with sound and heat; shrieks and screams so loud they made the ground shake. The winner was never in doubt and, as I watched, the larger shape began to spin faster and faster, while the smaller crawled toward where I stood in the shadow of my apple tree. The earth opened beneath the spinning shape and it vanished down into a chasm, which closed behind it leaving a perfect circle of greying ash.

The other daemon, my daemon, stretched out one scaly hand toward me, the claws broken, one of the seven fingers missing. "Help!" It was a whisper on the air but the breath behind it curled the leaves above me.

"How do I help you? What can I do?"

There was no reply and I realised my visitor had passed out. For a fleeting second I thought of calling an ambulance. I even had my phone in my hand, but then I realised the crew would have no more idea of how to help him than I did.

After a few seconds the daemon stirred. "I'm so cold." He began to shiver. Was he slipping into shock? I'd done basic first aid, but none of the rules would apply here.

Perhaps I should try to get him warm? "I'll fetch you a blanket."

He struggled to sit up. "No use. It would only burn. I need real heat. How about a bushel of coals from your fire?"

"Erm, I don't have any coal. I only have a gas fire."

As another shiver passed through him, his torn and twisted wings rattled like twigs in a storm.

I looked around me. "I do have a barbecue though. And I'm sure there's a bag of charcoal in the garage."

"Ah yes, that might help. We have lots of barbecues at home."

I hoped I only imagined him smacking his lips.

It took a while to produce enough heat. By that stage I was becoming much more concerned. The tip of the daemon's forked tail had changed from a deep cherry red to a muddy brown.

"I'll go and make us a nice pot of tea. I'm sure a warm drink will make you feel better. It always works for me."

"Stewed leaves in water? Ugh, no. I don't mind the occasional sip of boiling oil but that's all." He lifted one of his broken wings and peered at the damage. "I can't fly."

"No, but maybe it'll mend."

"I don't think so." He closed his golden eyes. "I can't stay here."

"I don't think you'd get far if you tried to leave."

"No, I wouldn't." There was silence for a moment. "Have you anything I could eat?"

"What do you like? I've got some ham, a bit of salad..."

"More leaves! No, what I'd like is a bit of brimstone."

"Brimstone? I've heard of it, but I'm not sure what it is or where to get hold of it."

"Sullllphurrrr!" The word echoed round the garden, the long drawn out L and the rolling R more like muffled thunder than letters of the alphabet.

"Right. The stuff that smells like rotten eggs?"

"Hmmm! What could be more enticing?"

I could think of a lot of things. And I still had no idea where to get what he needed. With no great hope of success I had a look online.

"Well, what do you know? I can get it. They add it to roses and it's £25.97 for 25 kilos. Mind you, it'll take a few days to arrive. I've not got Prime."

"It's now I'm hungry!"

"I know. Tell you what. I'll drive out to the local garden centre. You wait here."

"Where else can I go? They don't want me at home." He gave a loud sniff.

The garden centre staff gave me an odd look as I loaded seven boxes of sulphur treatment into my trolley. I tried telling them I had several acres of roses but I don't think they believed me. I would have to go somewhere else when this supply ran out. Not to mention, helping the daemon was proving to be an expensive good deed.

It wasn't as if he appreciated it either. "Rubbish sulllphurrr, this. They wouldn't serve it at home."

"Well, you're not at home, are you?"

I watched him as he manoeuvred his shredded wings into new positions. They had a dull sheen to them, nothing like the red scales which covered most of the rest of him. "What are they made of?"

"A kind of living metal." He pointed a claw at what might have been his chest. "This is all best quality clay. Stands up to anything. Nothing like that feeble stuff you're made of."

Interesting. I had wondered why the wings made a sound like jangling wires when the shreds clanged together.

"Do they hurt?"

"Nah, I don't feel pain. It would get in the way when we're stuffing…" He broke off. "Never mind what we do."

For a while we sat in silence. It began to rain. I was worried the daemon would get cold again, even catch a chill, but the water evaporated with a loud sizzle as though it were skittering across a hot frying pan.

On the third day I had a brilliant idea. "I think I know someone who might be able to mend your wings."

He was sceptical and unhappy when I said I needed to photograph him. He was unfamiliar with the idea and worried other people might find out about him. I thought he was afraid someone might try to put him in a cage but it wasn't that.

He shook his head when I suggested it. "No, humans don't scare me. But Hell wouldn't like it. They'd send someone to finish me off." He raked a claw against the open bag of sulphur. "Promise me if they do, you won't plant roses in me. I can't stand roses. It's the smell, you know."

"They would bury you here?"

"What? No, I told you. I'm made of best clay, I am. Daemons don't have souls, don't have anything. I'd be just a bit of dirt."

"I'm sorry to hear that. So you're saying there isn't any point in my friend mending your wings, are you?"

"No, I'm not saying that at all. If I could fly again, I could go home. They'd let me in if I wasn't damaged."

I took the photograph to my friend, Rick. He's a welder. Though he wishes he was a sculptor.

He stared at Blizzard's likeness. "Who made this? It's amazing. Reminds me of an Anthony Gormley, though it's not so much the Angel of the North, more like the Daemon of the South."

"Yes, but can you see it's not complete?"

He peered at the wings for a long moment. "You want me to finish it?"

"If you can. But, Rick, don't tell anyone. It'll be our secret until it's ready to exhibit."

He came round after work with a little solder kit and a bag of scrap. He had assumed the photograph had been of a tiny model, not a daemon as large as Blizzard. Not to mention it had never crossed his mind the creature might be alive.

When he had recovered from his shock, which took quite a while and a couple of beers, he had Blizzard stretch out the injured wings so he could see the extent of the damage. "I could weld patches and strips of steel onto you, but it couldn't be done here. I can't bring the equipment and the amount of metal we're going to need out of the garage. I'll fetch the truck round and we'll move you once the streets are quiet."

Two o'clock in the morning and Blizzard was sitting on the oil stained floor of Rick's place of work. He liked it.

And when Rick started up his welding equipment, liked it even more. Far from hurting him the sparks blended into his skin and he purred like some giant, scaly cat. His tail lost the grey tinge and he grinned at us.

"This is better, more like home."

Rick worked for over an hour. The right wing was now more silver steel than strange, dull living metal.

Taking a break, Rick sat beside me on an old bench close to Blizzard. "There is one problem, you know. I'm using a lot of steel and someone will have to pay for it. I don't suppose..."

I bit my lip. "I've no money. I'm only just managing to keep our friend here in sulphur."

Blizzard turned his head and two brilliant, golden eyes observed us. "Money is no problem for me. How much would you like? The last financial situation I sorted out was a mere two million and a yacht the guy couldn't even sail. I'd advise, in the current economic climate, you ask for... hmm... twenty million? It's a nice round number."

Rick leaned forward. "You can give us some money? Twenty million? Where would you get that?"

Blizzard scratched his long nose. "Not your problem. Well, is twenty enough?"

"Oh yes, I'd be happy with half that."

Why was I not surprised when a long piece of paper appeared in the air in front of Rick?

"Just sign it at the bottom. There's no need to concern yourself with the details. They're not very interesting."

"I don't have a pen."

Blizzard laughed. "You don't need one. Just use your finger. You'll feel a little prick but it won't hurt much."

"Stop!" I jumped to my feet and batted the paper away. "I know what this is. It's a contract with the devil for Rick's soul. Do you deny it?"

"Why would I? After all, it's what I do. In the end I'm just one more hard working salesman."

"My soul?" Rick also jumped to his feet. "How underhand of you. Trying to trick me, eh? Well, I'm not going to do any more welding for you, mate. What's more, I'm going to phone the press. They'll find you fascinating."

"All right, no contract." Blizzard pointed at the floating paper, which burst into flames and showered us all in ash. "Tell you what. I'll give you a freebie."

There was a soft thud over to my right and a briefcase was lying on the workshop floor.

Rick made no move to touch it. "What are you up to now?"

"Nothing. It's a gift: some free money, about twenty thousand. It's owner lost it so you can have it. But do finish my wings, please!"

The case was locked but it was the work of a few moments to lever it open. Inside were bundles of crisp, new twenty pound notes tied up with rubber bands.

"No contract?"

"That's what I promised. I wouldn't do anything like that to you, Rick. You're my friend." He grinned at us, displaying a mouthful of jagged, uneven teeth.

I glanced at Rick, who shrugged.

Another hour and the work was completed. I couldn't help dreaming of paying off my arrears and perhaps even treating myself to a shopping spree.

Blizzard pirouetted, preening himself in the wing mirror of an old Ford Escort. "Nice, very nice. You know this could start a trend. When they see mine everyone will want steel tips."

"What are you going to do now?"

He bowed his head to me. "Now I will return to Hell. I thank you for showing me the hospitality of your home and look forward to extending to you the hospitality of mine in due course."

He began to spin, his wings wrapping round him as he swirled. In seconds he was gone straight down through the workshop floor, leaving only a dark burn to show he had ever been there.

Rick picked up the briefcase. "We'll split this, after expenses, of course. And then I'm off to book a long holiday."

We never saw Blizzard again, but there has been a constant stream of other visitors. Who would have guessed the inhabitants of Hell would be so fashion conscious? All work is on a strict no contract basis, to be paid for in cash or in kind as soon as it's completed.

After a while we began to worry in case we ran out of clients. There must be a limit to the number of daemons, but then this morning...

She says white is soooo boring. What she wants is steel tipped flight feathers.

And who are we to argue?

LIME TREE ARBOUR

My fingers slipped on the padlock key. My hands were shaking. I couldn't believe I was doing this. I had never done anything illegal before, never had so much as a parking ticket, yet here I was breaking into this lock-up. I wasn't sure it even belonged to the man I was planning to bury in the lime tree arbour but I hoped it did because, if it did, all I had to do was remove a package from the glove compartment of the car inside and I would be eight thousand pounds better off.

The money, if it was there at all, was the proceeds of a robbery gone wrong. My Uncle George and his two mates, Chris and Eric, stole it from a swanky jewellers in town. The manager interrupted them as they were taking the contents out of the safe. Startled, George shot him as the three robbers fled. At least they remembered to take the money and the jewels with them.

Before he died, the manager gave the police a pretty good description of George. He wasn't hard to recognise anyway, what with his scarred face and his crooked smile.

When they tracked him down he was stupid. He ought to have raised his arms but he didn't. The police thought he was reaching for a gun so they shot him. It turned out later he had been unarmed.

I didn't attend the funeral. He had been from the wrong side of the family. He had spent more time in prison than out. I wasn't even supposed to know anything about him but years ago I had found the stash of letters my mother kept hidden. George wanted someone to boast to and his sister was the one he had chosen: little Julia, good, straight-as-they-come Julia. She had no idea I had read every one of his words, shivering with delight and awe at George's descriptions of the terrible crimes he claimed to have committed.

It was only natural my mother would be upset by her brother's death but she was far too respectable to want to be seen mourning him. My father was relieved when she decided not go to the funeral. I think I was the only one who shed any tears. My secret hero was gone. There would be no more exciting instalments in the long running saga of Uncle George and his band of daring robbers.

I decided I would sneak out to the place where he had been buried. I couldn't figure out how to go about stealing a wreath so instead I took some of our neighbour's prize winning roses and my mother's favourite painted porcelain vase.

The graveyard was empty, no visitors on that cold, dank afternoon. I wasn't sure where, amongst the many tumbled and handful of upright stones, I would find George's grave. I looked around for signs of earth turned over in recent days. I doubted he would have much of a headstone.

"You looking for me, Lucy?"

The voice made me jump. I turned.

My Uncle George was sitting on the low wall surrounding a line of dustbins. I recognised him from the single photograph my mother had kept. He looked no older than he had in that image, which must have been taken twenty years earlier.

"Uncle George!" I was delighted. The stupid police must have got it wrong, though I did wonder who they had shot and buried in place of my relative.

He nodded at the flowers. "Those are nice. Shall we put them on my grave? I didn't get many, you know, and not one single rose, not even from Jools."

"I suppose we might." I had to do something with the wilting blooms. I couldn't take them back, could I?

He led me to a shady corner some distance from the chapel.

I peered down at an insignificant mound of damp, grey clay. "Who's really in there?"

"What do you mean?"

"I mean, who did they bury instead of you?"

He jerked back and stared at me. "You think I'm still alive, do you? Ah, you haven't realised..." He laughed.

"Stop it, Uncle George. I'm not a child. I don't believe in ghosts."

"Your choice, I guess, but I'm not going to walk through a wall to prove you're wrong. I'm going to do something much more useful." He leaned over me. "You see, I hid the diamonds. If I tell you where they are, you can see Chris and Eric get their shares, can't you? My cut of the money is no use to me now but you..." He cocked his head to one side. "I'm sure you could make good use of it."

He had me there. With enough money, I could chuck up my boring job and leave this God forsaken town behind me. And my parents wouldn't be able to tell me what to do any more. All right, he could pretend to be a ghost if he liked. He wasn't fooling me. "Why not? You tell me where to find the loot and I'll go and fetch it."

"Not so fast, my dear. There is one other thing." He waved his arm over the mound. "I don't like it here. I want you to move me."

A shiver passed through me. My legs came close to giving way. I could see the flowers I had placed beside the hump of earth but I saw them through the faint outline of Uncle George's hand, his fingers now as insubstantial as the air. I think I may have passed out for a second or two.

George was leaning over me again. He was muttering something about, "...nervous women. Should have picked a feller."

"No! No, you shouldn't. I'll get the jewels."

"OK and you'll move me to the lime tree arbour?"

"If that's what you want."

"Good girl. Now, you'll need money and some transport."

For a second I thought he meant I was to borrow the family car. I experienced a sudden vision of me trying to explain to my father how the boot came to be full of mud.

"Pay attention, Lucy. All you have to do is find out what the police did with the keys I had in my pocket when they shot me. I've been renting a lock-up, you see."

I was sure he already knew my mother, as his nearest relative, had been given everything the police had found in his possession. She had bundled it all together and thrown it into a box at the back of the garage. She said it would have been disrespectful to get rid of it so soon after George had passed away. My father disagreed.

George told me where the lock-up was and sent me on my way. By the time I was half way home I had almost managed to convince myself I had only imagined meeting him. Almost but not quite.

I found the keys among George's effects. They were in the pocket of his overcoat, the one with the rust coloured stain high on the left side next to the top button. There were six keys in all. Two I knew belonged to the flat he had rented. The landlady had opted to change the locks rather than have them back. She had said she wanted no reminders of that rogue. One, I was surprised to realise, was a spare belonging to my family's house. Had George visited when we were out? If he had, I was certain my father could not have known. Two of the other three looked like they belonged to padlocks, while the final one was quite small. I guessed that one maybe fitted a suitcase.

I stuffed everything except the keys back into the box. It was already getting late. I would have to leave finding the lock-up until the next morning.

The building was a surprise. I'd expected to find a tumbledown lean-to packed with cardboard boxes full of dubious electrical goods and similar items of plunder. It turned out I had been watching too many police dramas. It was one of a set of modern, brick built garages with a cream coloured up-and-over door. I turned the key in the lock, pushed at the panel and went inside. There was a light switch on the wall to my right. I tried it. It worked. I reminded myself, Uncle George had been dead for less than a month.

Most of the space was taken up by a car. It was an old, red, nineteen-sixties mini, which wouldn't have been out of place in *The Italian Job*, except the paintwork on this one was scratched all over. I tried the driver's door and it was was unlocked. There was a key on the seat. I picked it up, got in and used it to open the glove compartment. Inside was a wrapped package.

A few minutes of counting later I discovered I was now the undisputed owner of just over eight thousand pounds, more money than I had ever seen in my entire life.

A thought crossed my mind. What if I didn't go back to the churchyard? What could dear, dead George do to me if I took this cash and decided not to honour his request?

Ah but... simple greed consumed me. Eight thousand was a drop in the ocean when compared to the value of what he had stolen in the jewellery heist. Eight thousand wouldn't buy me a place of my own. It wasn't even enough to let me quit my job.

The next day I rang in sick and returned to George's grave.

Following George's instructions, I made contact with Chris. I told him nothing about ghosts and never even hinted I might know where the jewels had been hidden. All I did was pay him the five hundred pounds he demanded for helping me move my uncle to the arbour.

After we had reburied the body and Chris had left, George reappeared. He told me to start digging beneath another of the lime trees then vanished again. I soon discovered a rucksack about two feet down stuffed with rings, bracelets and a lot of loose gemstones.

It was at that point it dawned on me I had no idea how to turn this glittering cascade into hard cash. I wondered if I could just turn up at a pawnbrokers. There was one I knew of in the town. "We buy your gold," it proclaimed on a huge banner above the window. But once again I had seen enough police dramas to be aware most of the local pawnbrokers would be on the lookout for gems as hot as these. I walked over to George's new resting place and sat on the damp grass.

After a while I sensed someone watching me. I wasn't surprised. He was perched on a bench at the centre of the arbour. "You didn't listen, Lucy. I said you could have my share, not all of the loot. You'll need Chris's help again. Go and tell him I sent you a letter with instructions on what to do if anything happened to me."

Chris was drinking tea in the same cafe where I had found him the first time. I showed him the rucksack and he recognised it at once.

"How did you get hold of this?"

I don't think he was at all convinced by my tale about a posthumous letter. I knew as soon as I handed the bag over he intended to cheat me but what could I do about it?

I headed straight back to George. He wasn't surprised either but said he had to give Chris at least a chance but now Chris had blown it.

"You'll have to kill him, pet."

"What? Don't be ridiculous. I can't do that."

"Why not? It's not as hard as you think. I know where he'll go with the jewels and that fence is a shifty bugger. Chris getting shot on his premises won't raise an eyebrow. You can bring the gems back here. Oh and why don't I just..." He vanished again.

I sat on the bench wishing I had never got involved.

Overnight I replayed everything in my head. How dare Chris behave like this to me? I had as much right to George's share as he had, more in fact, since George himself had told me I could have it.

The next morning I went back to the arbour. I had decided I would have to tell George there was nothing I could do, even though I would have liked to teach Chris a lesson. I didn't have a clue how to get hold of a gun, let alone how to use one.

George pulled a face. "Use your imagination, girl. What do you think I did with the gun that killed the manager? That's the one we'll use on Chris."

I told myself it was all nonsense. If I had a gun, I was sure all I would need to do was threaten Chris and he would see sense and give me George's share.

The weapon was in the last place anyone would have thought to look. George had used his key to enter my parents' house while they were out and had hidden the weapon under the floorboards of my bedroom. Long before I was born, he said, the room had been his.

When he was seventeen he had cut the hole out and re-covered it. It became the place where he hid his first stashes. Somehow this new connection made us closer than before.

He was right when he said recovering the weapon posed no risk to me at all. Anyway, I had no intention of using it. After I had sorted Chris out, I would bury the gun beside my uncle.

After a week George told me the time was right. Chris had made contact with the fence and that evening they were going to agree a price for the jewels.

The night was cold and dark, no moon and, since the recent cuts, only one in three street lights were switched on. It was simple enough for me to avoid the scattered pools of pale light. By now I knew they didn't matter at all to George. As far as I could tell, no one else could see or hear him.

The gun poked me in the side through the pocket of the ample coat he had instructed me to buy. These days he often came with me when I left the lime grove as he was no longer held in place by the constraints of sacred ground, since there was nothing holy at all about the arbour.

He passed right through the door of the fence's dwelling and was back in seconds. "No problem. They're in the far room having a drink before getting down to business."

"I'm not going to hurt anyone."

"Of course you're not. Now, come on. Do like I showed you."

His lock picks were already in my hand. He had trained me, not the easiest of tasks when he could not demonstrate, but I listened to his instructions, practised on every door I could find. He was pleased with my progress, said I was a natural just like he used to be. The levers shifted and there was the softest of clicks. An owl seeking its prey would have made more sound.

Into the hallway and a light showed under a door to my right. Two voices, laughter, the clink of metal on wood.

"You did well, even better than I was expecting. I can give you a good price for all of these."

"Yeah, everyone thought old George was the brains but he weren't."

George bristled. "I'll show them who was the brains."

He flickered and was beside me again. "Their backs are to us, Lucy. We won't get a better chance. In we go!"

He passed through at the same instant I shoved the door open. Chris and another man swung round to look at me. "Who are you?"

"She's Lucy, George's niece." Chris dropped the gems and took a step toward me. "What are you doing here?"

"Who cares what she's doing. We can't let her go now. She'll bring the police." The other man swung his fist at me.

Everything happened so fast. I didn't mean to use the gun. I didn't mean to fire at him and then at Chris. It wasn't my fault. I'm not to blame. I only did what George had taught me, one long afternoon in the lime tree arbour.

I was surprised how little I felt as I stared down on the two sprawled bodies. I scooped up the jewels from the table. They didn't quite fill the rucksack.

George was across the room from me. "Come on, Lucy. Get this open." He was leaning against a huge, old safe.

"Don't be ridiculous. We'd need a ton of explosives."

"You could always try the combination."

"How would you know that?"

He tapped his nose. "Can't you guess?"

It wasn't difficult. "You watched the fence opening it."

"I did and now it's our turn."

Inside were bundles of notes and several velvet cases. He told me not to touch anything except the money.

As we left the shop behind us, I realised I was rich. I had got away with the perfect crime. Why would anyone suspect me?

And why stop at this? I could have a whole new career, aided and abetted by my dear, late uncle. It's true I had never met George in the flesh but I had a feeling I was going to be spending a lot of time with him in the lime tree arbour.

INK

Ink was invented by the devil in an idle hour. The concept was so simple and so diabolical his tail curled up in delight and a stray tendril of smoke escaped, strengthening the delicious whiff of sulphur in the air around him.

Before this there had only been paint and brushes. Pictures told limited tales. Even those drawn by the clever Egyptians were a clumsy way to convey information. Years of training were needed to be able to replicate and interpret the stories being told. To the uninitiated they were a secret code.

Communication was by word and words were often forgotten. It was true there were messengers who covered miles to convey accurate information. In Greece, Pheidippides broke records with his Marathon run but most messages twisted as they travelled the short distance from mouth to mouth. It wasn't so easy to start a war or break a lover's heart. If more mischief were to be possible, some better method of recording speech was required.

Satan's first experiments were with blood. He liked the colour and it had a certain binding effect if the donor was alive when the document was signed.

It was unfortunate but it wasn't available in sufficient quantities on a day to day basis. Besides, he intended his new invention to be used by all those in power and too many were squeamish or nervous given such an obvious a sign of his involvement. In order to have any great effect, ink must be seen as a pleasant, innocuous substance.

He sat for a while beneath an oak tree and observed his favourite insects, the wasps, as they flew in and out of the branches. Too lazy and solitary to work together to make nests as the bees did, they would burrow into the tree to make a hole for their larvae. In self defence, the injured tree would scab over the cavity. People called the scabs oak apples or galls. They would often destroy them, knowing what was developing inside. No one except the devil had a fondness for the wasps. He'd had a soft spot for them ever since he realised they could with a simple sting make the most polite person use oaths of a most ungodly nature. He saw a way to help his little friends.

He whispered in the ears of sleeping monks, "Try the liquid left in the gall after the wasp has flown." Unsure where they had got the inspiration to do so, they did. It was not long before the monasteries were overflowing with ink.

He didn't care for the use the monks made of his invention: the pretty illustrated books full of bible stories and the lives of saints. For a while he sulked and spat brimstone at the walls of Hell but soon realised it was a small price to pay for the spread of his new medium.

Kings learned it was a more effective way to declare war on their neighbours. There could be no room for doubt. A spoken insult could be brushed off. "He doesn't mean it. It's being misinterpreted. I'll send a runner with a box of gold to check" became, "How dare he write this? Fetch my armour. Summon my men!"

Scribes were trained to add up columns of figures and show the results and the first tax demand was produced. The devil began to receive recognition for his work as people often used his name when they were given one.

Another enterprising king used his ink to make a list of everything owned by the people he had just conquered: so much easier to claim it all as his.

Oh, the unhappiness ink was causing. Squabbles over land became ever more serious as boundaries were noted; made permanent.

Using ink gave people a sense of importance. The sin of pride was much in evidence. Signing death warrants was a singular pleasure for some, giving way to prejudice, avarice and hate. Murder by proxy.

Best of all were the lies told on paper. Even the devil was amazed at the way the people believed any nonsense so long as it was written in ink. See it twice and it was an indisputable fact mere logical words could not overcome. Some scribes became famous. They learned that the more lurid and rude a tale, the more people wanted to read it. Truth was the first victim of the widespread use of ink. All Hell rejoiced.

Not all the devil's triumphs were on so large a scale. Foolish people would insist on using ink to confess to themselves. The diary was born. When it was found by someone else, trouble often ensued.

Then there was the last will and testament. Before, succession was a simple matter. Everyone knew what to expect but now it became complex. A landowner could sow seeds of mistrust between his children with threats of leaving his belongings to the one he preferred. A pot of ink became a weapon able to split a family.

Those with little courage found a way to end an affair without having to act as though they too were broken hearted. The suicide note was often not so much an explanation as a way of apportioning guilt and spreading unhappiness.

Betrayal became easy. Ink lasted. Letters from lovers were permanent, kept to read again. An unfortunate queen saved hers in a secret chest. When it was discovered, her cousin had her beheaded. The devil laughed.

Everything was going so well. Ink was a division between people. The ability to use it gave status and could be the road to wealth. Wealth led to bad behaviour, envy, thievery, gluttony... all to the devil's delight and an increase in the population of his domain. Until... the angels got involved. It was Satan's own fault. He had stolen a few long, white plumes from a wing while its owner was busy playing her harp. He thought they would make a beautiful set of quills as a present for a king who had started his third war in as many years. The angel was upset at the hole in her flight feathers and complained to her boss.

Satan's invention was noticed.

It was not an easy problem to solve. Ink had now been around for a long time. To take it away at this point could be seen as interfering in free will since lots of decisions had been made regarding how to use the substance. Like the good fairy in the story of Sleeping Beauty, they could not cancel out what had been done but it was possible to mitigate the effects.

Education was the answer. Teach everyone to use ink. The more people who could write and read, the more dilute the evil would become. Letters could be written to argue against injustice. Discussion could take place between people who had never met. Pamphlets could be produced giving other views, on war, on slavery, on how life should be lived. The powerful would lose a weapon from their overstocked armoury.

It would no longer be "publish and be damned". It would be "publish and be blessed."

In hell the devil cursed. He would never have started this had he known it would lead to: Magna Carta, Thomas Paine's Rights of Man, William Wilberforce and Elizabeth Fry, even the American Declaration of Independence. Now the downtrodden and wronged of the earth could draw attention to injustice and begin to fight for their rights!

He would have written a long diatribe on the subject but the ink evaporated and the paper burst into flames in the hot fires of hell.

FATE IS A SPINDLE CARVED FROM OLIVE WOOD

She has two sisters but she never intended me to meet them. She said I wouldn't like them and they would hate me. Yet early each morning off she went to work with them, returning only as darkness fell. She refused to discuss what she did all day, saying it was too boring and wouldn't interest me. I guessed she worked in the office, perhaps managing the personnel in the factory she owned together with her siblings. It had been inherited from their parents and was a strange, old building, a long, low structure uncomfortably sandwiched between crumbling office blocks in the unfashionable part of town. The once gilded but now faded letters above the door announced it was the "Moirai Spinning Company Ltd." The business had been started many years earlier when her family came over from Greece, the only trace of that heritage still remaining being the odd names of the sisters.

I engineered my first meeting with her. I was employed as a representative of an importer of raw silk and we were seeking new outlets. There are not many spinners of natural threads left. These days the public is too ready to embrace cheap synthetics. I had high hopes of success with the company as I could find no trace of any existing contracts others had with them, yet the factory must have been spinning something or it would long ago have gone out of business. I was in a position to offer them a deal I was convinced could not be bettered.

That day I hung around outside the factory and observed the double doors. At five o'clock Clotho emerged and I intercepted her as she strode over to her bright red Porsche. "Excuse me? I wonder if I could have a word with you."

"Make an appointment."

"I've tried but I can't get through. No one ever answers the phone."

She turned to look at me.

Our eyes met and every thought in my head evaporated.

She hesitated, her hand halfway to the door. The keys fell to the ground. We bumped heads as we both reached for them.

"Perhaps I might have a few minutes."

I knew a few minutes would never be enough. "What about dinner?" I couldn't believe I had said the words... or the smile with which she greeted them.

"Why not? There's a little restaurant I like to frequent but it's on the other side of town. Though I must warn you I never discuss business in the evenings." She stepped into the car and the passenger door seemed to open without her touching it.

I can't remember what we ate but I do remember she was right. We didn't discuss contracts, not then or at any other time.

We went out together every night for the next few weeks and later on she moved in with me. At first everything was wonderful, the only downside being the way my employer kept on about how I should be using my influence with her to land that major contract he needed. "Silk doesn't sell itself," he said. "You're way behind target and slipping further down the league table." I knew it was a threat but when I was with her nothing else mattered.

When at last I did mention it she laughed. "I don't deal with that side of things. All I do is organise the spinning." Her voice dropped to a whisper. "My sister, Lachesis, is the allotter but she won't speak to you. She knows I'm involved with someone and she's jealous. And Atropos never listens to anyone anyway. She has her ways and she never changes her mind. Lachesis and I call her 'Sister Inflexible'."

"Maybe if I were to speak to her, show her some samples?"

"No. You will not go near either of my sisters. I forbid it." In that instant she was as distant from me as the stars. There was a tone in her voice I had never heard before. I didn't want to admit it but she scared me.

By the next morning the fear was gone. Only anger remained. Who was she to say I could not speak to her sisters? What harm could it do? It wasn't as though I was about to leave her.

I waited until her Porsche was out of sight then I picked up my case of samples and followed her. I didn't want a row but the pressure from my boss was becoming unbearable. I hadn't landed a single new contract since Clotho and I had become an item.

I had to try to speak to her sisters. But how to get to them without her knowing? I was sure, once the deed was done, she would come round. But for now I had to bypass her. I couldn't risk involving a receptionist and I had no idea of the layout of the factory, though I guessed it would be similar to others I had visited. Perhaps it was a little unorthodox but I avoided the main door and, keeping close to the wall beneath the windows, made my way to the rear of the building.

I discovered the doors that should have admitted goods arriving on lorries were all locked and chained. Neither were there any recent tyre tracks in the mud outside the loading bay, not even any empty cages that might have contained raw material. There was no one around at all and the windows were grimy and covered in cobwebs. I couldn't hear any sound from inside. I had never come across any kind of spinning machine capable of making so little noise. There wasn't even the steady hum of generated current. It was as though the factory was abandoned, disused.

I found a cracked pane and pushed at the glass. There was little resistance. It fell inside with a crash and I held my breath as I waited for someone to come and investigate.

After nothing happened for several minutes I eased the remainder of the pane out of the way and clambered inside. I knew it was the wrong thing to do but by that stage I had already forgotten the reason for my visit. I was consumed with curiosity.

Where there should have been busy workers there wasn't a living soul. There was no machinery either. Nothing. Only a dusty floor and an open door.

I found myself in a corridor. It was so quiet I could hear my footsteps echoing through the building.

It was then it dawned on me. I had never seen anyone except the three sisters enter or emerge from the factory. Did they have any workers at all?

Two more doors and I gasped as I gazed down from a circular balcony onto a scene in a central open area several floors beneath me. Whatever I might have expected to find, it would never have been this. The floor of the room was covered in stubby grass and in the centre was a small olive grove. Beneath the trees, on three small stools, sat the three sisters.

They were so absorbed in what they were doing they did not see me. Indeed, the scene was so unreal it took a while for me to comprehend what was happening. It was all so bizarre. Clotho held a spindle and from mid air produced a shining, gilded thread. There was no basket of raw material, no place for the substance to be coming from, yet it was there. Her sister, Lachesis, held in her hands a golden rod with which she measured the thread and every few seconds Atropos would wield a pair of silver shears, cutting through the measured thread in one precise motion. The severed piece would float in the air for the briefest instant before vanishing.

I must have made a sound. All three jerked their heads to look up at me. Their faces twisted, their mouths opened in identical snarls. For a second I saw not three young women but three hideous crones as old as time itself.

I fled, running as fast as I could back the way I had come. I made it to the window and out across the deserted loading area, the one which had never been necessary.

I skidded onto the street and, to my amazement, Clotho was there, holding open the door of her Porsche. "Get in! They don't know who you are yet but they'll soon work it out."

We raced across the city and out into the countryside. We didn't stop until the car was almost out of fuel. I had no idea where we were. We rested overnight in a nondescript motel and in the morning set out again.

Since then our flight has continued; one city, one country after another. Clotho always has money and we are managing to stay ahead of her searching sisters. I know it cannot go on for much longer. I am mortal. Somewhere the thread she once spun, its length the span of my life, is out of sight, out of reach, twined in her long, silken hair.

"Where will you lead me next?"

She names somewhere I have never heard of, one more place in which many threads are gathered, a place she can hide a chosen one.

While he remains her chosen one...

How long has it been since we fled the factory? How long have we travelled together? It could be as short as an hour or as long as eternity. I find it hard to remember a life before she entered mine.

I am no fool. I know she will tire of me. The time will come when she returns to her siblings. I am no more than a dalliance, a holiday, and I'm sure there were others before me, as there will be others after me.

I look at the tight braids around her forehead and at her curling tresses. How many threads is she hiding in there? If I touched it, would I recognise my own?

I'm tired now. I've tried to bore her, to persuade her it is time to let her sisters catch up with us but she only laughs and teases me.

From beneath the pillow she withdraws her spindle carved from ancient olive wood, the one she has tried so often to lose or to give away but which she knows will never allow itself to leave her side.

I snatch at her hair. A thread comes away, lying snaked in my palm; a coil of shining life. I cannot straighten it as it does not yet have an end.

Her eyes narrow but then, as though I have done this only to amuse her, she laughs. "Do you want to kill him?"

"Who is he?" I stare into her eyes. "Is he me?"

She shrugs and more threads as delicate as the finest silk scatter over her shoulder. "We could always find out."

We have tarried too long this time. I hear a knocking at the door. Beyond it wait Lachesis with her rod and Atropos with her silver shears.

But am I brave enough to offer up this thread, this life, to their measurement? Is it even mine to yield?

AFTER SCARLET IN THE MOONLIGHT

"You can still change your mind. I'm not putting pressure on you." Lynn's fingers sift through the small mountain of pills, caressing each one as though it were a diamond.

But she's lying. Putting pressure on me is her only function.

"Are you certain the sales forecasts can't be wrong?"

"There's a tiny chance you might pull off some kind of coup but it's..." She holds up her hand, thumb and forefinger pressed close together, a hairsbreadth of light between them. "...infinitesimal. And it won't be with us."

She's told me this already. The record company are set to drop me. The success of *Scarlet In The Moonlight* will be impossible to repeat. The pinnacle of my career is now behind me. If I continue making music, all that awaits me is a steady decline into obscurity. One hit wonders are just that: there for a fleeting moment, a firework brighter than the sun. Then gone. Lynn had come to offer me the chance of immortality. I would join the estimable company of those brilliant performers whose lives ended at the peak of their dreams. The roll call of accidents and suicides. Fame coming at the ultimate price.

But the alternative? Would I want to continue living when no one recognised me any longer?

"It won't hurt a bit."

"How do you know that?"

She laughs. "Come on. We know our substances. Haven't we kept you on the right side of them for long enough?"

I can't deny the fact, though I wish I could.

The pills call to me. I haven't asked what they are. Probably a cocktail designed for maximum effect in the minimum time. Lynn will want my body to be discovered ready for the six o'clock news. No doubt the downloads are all prepared, the memorabilia printed. There will be a short period during which the world will go insane. Everyone will want a piece of me. The record company will want to be positioned to take advantage. Yes, the maximum effect in the minimum time.

All my life I've desired fame. It took so long to get here. I can't let it vanish now. I reach out for...

"I wouldn't do that if I were you."

My hand jerks back. A tall, dark haired man stands beside the door. I didn't hear him enter and there's something odd about him. It's as though he's just a little out of focus.

"Who are you?"

"A well wisher who doesn't want to see you doing something you'll regret for a very long time."

Lynn waves her hand in front of my face. "Who are you talking to?" She peers at the doorway. "Had you already taken something before I got here?"

"Is this man not with you, then?"

"What man? There's only us here. Do you imagine I'd have brought a witness?"

The stranger shrugs. "She can't see me. It's better that way. I'll be in enough trouble if my bosses find out I've had a chat with you. I don't want to make things any worse."

I must be hallucinating. There's no other possibility. Drugs can do that to you. The only problem is I've been clean for weeks.

The stranger walks across to the table. "Take these and your death will be an agony but I promise you it's nothing compared to what will follow."

"She says they won't hurt me."

"She lies. And you know it."

Lynn is all big round eyes and her face has gone pale. "Are you insane? There is no one in this room except you and me. Stop playing the fool and get on with it."

I'm wondering what game these two are playing when my visitor brings his hand down on top of the pills. And it passes straight through them and the table beneath.

"Get the picture now?"

"You... You're a ghost!" A sudden cold grips me and I fall back onto the arm of the chair.

Lynn crushes her lips together. "I've had enough of this. If you won't get on with it because you've turned coward on me, I understand. But do stop pretending you're seeing things. It's childish."

"I'm not seeing things. There's a man standing by the table. He's telling me not to go through with this."

"A man? Right. Here, is he?" She stomps round the table. My visitor turns toward her and blows on her hair. I see strands of it move around her ears.

She shivers. "This room is draughty. But there are only the two of us here."

He blows on her again but the repetition doesn't help.

She grabs her bag. "I'm not staying. It's up to you. Your career is over either way. It's your choice whether the world remembers you or not. I didn't come here to murder you."

As she nears the door it swings open by itself. She hurries through and it closes behind her.

"Couldn't resist that," he says. "Now, about your future."

"What future? You heard her. I'm finished."

"I doubt that. You've just managed to evade your death. Not many people can say that."

"So I was supposed to die tonight?"

"Yes and I was supposed to collect you but it's a bit busy in Hell at the moment. I took a gamble on no one noticing if I interfered a little. You were down as a 'probable'. You still had a few minutes of free will left, balance sheet not quite complete, et cetera. Now you've time to alter your destiny. And your destination."

"I'll never be really famous, though, will I?"

"It's pretty unlikely but who knows? Well, I must be going. I do hope we don't meet again."

He is gone. The room is quiet. And I am left to ponder what life will be like if no one notices me any longer.

My eyes drift to the stack of pills.

G.W.O.T.W.

Can you hear me now? No more distractions? Good.

I apologise for the shock my colleague gave you but you have to admit it did the job. That tangled heap of glass and plastic won't make any more racket. Whatever made you choose that ringtone? There are so many less irritating ones.

Now to business. You must have learned the rules at school. "Don't write in the margins. Always use your ruler to create a nice, straight line down the side of your page." These are the instructions we have whispered into the ears of teachers for generations and until recent times it was enough. They passed them on and everyone followed suit.

The middle of the page is yours, the edges are ours. It solves two problems: your writing looks neater and we have space for ours. At first we used lemon juice. It gave such a nice, fresh tang. Even the most dusty, dry words smelled pleasant. These days it's all chemicals... when it happens at all, which brings me to my point.

We have always found supplies of unused paper to be a problem. The strongest of us can only move a few sheets at a time. Big rolls are impossible and we can't hijack delivery trucks from paper mills. We tried it a couple of times but in the crash the paper got wrecked, burnt or bled on.

We rely on people like yourself, who handwrite lots of letters, documents, even bills, all with margins but now what have you done? You've stopped buying letter paper. You "write" using computers.

Some of our members remember a time when a computer was a man who knew how to use an abacus. None of us are ready for the end of margins. We don't have less to pass on these days; if anything there is more. Bear in mind our numbers increase every hour.

It used to be easy. To cover a long distance, the information would be carried by one of us from one place to another then inscribed in the margin of a notice or an order. We thought you understood this. Why else are there margins, drawn with white or yellow lines, between the pavement and the road? We appreciate the gesture. It isn't comfortable having a car pass through you even if you can't feel anything.

You ask me what we want to communicate? That's obvious. Life doesn't end when you die. Well, it does but you know what I mean. We too have things to do, places to go. When you deprive us of a margin who knows the harm you do? It could have been a line of a play, a posthumous novel or a lonely hearts column. The possibilities are endless.

So next time you have the choice, consider us. Put that keyboard away and pick up your ruler. Become a good friend to the Ghost Writers Of The World.

CHOOSE NOW

Someone is in my room. I can feel their presence, though I didn't hear anyone come in. Not a creak from the old floor, not a click from a closing door. I'm sure they're standing beside my bed, watching me. They must have put the light on for I can sense a brightness through my eyelids. I don't want to open my eyes and admit I'm awake. It can only be one of the children trying to steal my last few minutes of peace before the alarm goes off. I have enjoyed them both coming to stay with me over my birthday weekend but we were up late last night, sitting round the fire, drinking too much wine, reminiscing about their childhoods.

Yes, they are pleasant company but it'll be a relief to wave them off back to their own homes and their own families. I so miss my routine.

I am a creature of habit. My alarm goes off at seven o'clock every morning, winter or summer. I get up, wrap my fluffy, purple dressing gown around me, pull on my slippers and leave the bedroom for the kitchen, where I press the button on the coffee machine. I turn on the fire in the living room (central heating is too expensive these days) and visit the bathroom. I collect the drinks for myself and Paul then take them back to bed where we stay until eight. How civilised.

I'm surprised the alarm hasn't gone off yet. It must be after seven by now. Ah, there it is, set to a light music channel as always. But today the tune is unfamiliar and the voice soars pure and sweeter than birdsong. If a precious gem had a sound, it would be like this. And the words… Was that my name?

I open my eyes. "What the…"

A figure stands between me and the door. I cannot make out any features and it is glowing, as though there is a pale star caught inside it.

"Time to get up, Jennifer. Time to leave."

I turn to Paul. "Wake up! There's a…" Words fail me.

Paul does not move. I cannot see him breathing. He is a statue beneath the covers. I put out my hand to shake him but there is a barrier; nothing I can see but my fingers curl inwards, the nails digging into my palms. I can't touch him.

"Oh, Paul." I shiver. "Is he dead?"

The figure reaches out to me. "No, Jennifer, he has more than a decade left in this world. It is you, my dear, who has just died. Now, come along with me. We should be on our way."

I rise from the bed. I am light, warm. It is years since I felt so well. And I know this creature, for there is something not quite human about it, is telling me the truth. I want to look round, to embrace Paul one last time, but already we are outside and the world is flying past us.

"Are you an angel?"

"Oh, no. I'm a lot further down than them. Not nearly so exalted. I'm only a humble facilitator. Don't worry. All will soon be clear."

Without any sense of transition I am in a room, an office. A mahogany desk stands in the centre with a chair on either side. As I cross the marble floor I become aware I am no longer wearing my plain cotton nightdress. It has been switched for a soft silk, calf length gown with a pattern of butterfly bright flowers, their stems entwined with emerald leaves. I remember it well. I wore it for my engagement party. I have never since possessed any garment I liked as much.

I take a seat at the desk and the figure perches on the one opposite. Now I have a clearer view of her, I see she is quite lovely. But, again, there is something unnatural about her. No mortal ever had eyes that colour, a face that shape. I try to peer round her, to find out if she has wings, but I don't think she does. And there's no sign of a harp. But, then again, she did say she was not an angel.

She opens a thick file which has appeared in front of her. "We are here to find your perfect moment, the one you will inhabit forever."

I can't think of any reply.

She turns the book to face me so I can see the title. My name is there and, written beneath it in deep gold letters at least a foot high, is "Seven a.m.".

"What does that mean?"

"Why, it's the time of day when you have most often been happy."

"Is that so?"

"It is. There is no doubt about it. You have experienced seven o'clock in the morning a total of 27,760 times, including the day when you managed to experience it twice. You have been happy on more than 8,020 of those occasions and supremely joyful on 2,262. Compare this with the figures for your least happy time of day, four-oh-five p.m., which has given you pleasure on only 52 occasions in your entire life."

"I see."

"No, you don't but you will. My job is to help you make a selection. Just one of those 2,262 memories will be yours to keep forever... to inhabit, if you will. Now, let's start narrowing it down, shall we? Would you like a coffee before we start? Or something stronger, perhaps?"

"Coffee, please." A familiar cup appears in front of me. The liquid inside is just the right colour and, when I taste it, for an instant I am once again a young student in the house of a friend. I have stayed overnight and her mother has created this sublime drink using fresh ground beans and a stove top percolator. Growing up I only ever had instant.

"There, now we are ready to begin." She taps the file. It shimmers and reveals the next page, on which is another set of numbers. The time has been joined by a date: 4th June 1953.

I am six. It is seven a.m. and I am wide awake. I run down the stairs, not that there is much to be excited about. Mummy and Daddy never listen to what I tell them. They will have bought me a silly doll and some crayons, not what I really want. Not a *bike*. Oh… it is! And it's the one from the shop in town. It's bright red and has stabilisers and a saddle and a basket and a bell and...

"No, not quite right. This day's very nice but you have had many better ones than this."

I shake myself. The memory had been so real.

The page is now swamped with colours, spinning and breaking apart like the kaleidoscope I was given by my grandma for Christmas when I was eight, a fleeting taste of sherbet on my tongue.

Now it is replaced by snow, pressed to my lips with gloved hands when, at seven a.m. on 15th January 1962 I sneak out of the house to build the world's best snowman with next door's children.

"Are you enjoying yourself, Jennifer?"

Her voice drags me back from feeding ducks with my parents the year before they divorced. "I think so."

"Don't worry. We've a long way to go yet and, when you find the right one, we'll both know. Shall we skip a few years?"

"Perhaps we better had." I don't need her to tell me there are few happy memories to be found in the dark, lean days after my father left and my mother nursed her bitterness. I was a lonely child; an angry child; a wayward child.

Scenes fly by.

Opening the envelope to find my exam results were good enough to take me to university, to escape from my clinging mother and my boring life in our small town.

Watching a vixen with her cubs crossing our garden on their way home through early morning mist.

Catching the ferry to France at seven a.m. on the 4th June 1965, excited at the prospect of the best birthday so far.

Then, on the table is a croissant, golden, crisp, irresistible, the scent spinning me into the arms of my first love. No, not Paul. He was later. This emotion is as powerful as an ocean wave but has the lasting depth of that same wave crashing onto the beach. It sinks into the sand with the salt flavour of tears... and is gone.

Paul has not been a wave but a rock. "What about the wedding? I loved that day."

"Yes, some of it. But the timing was wrong. Two-thirty p.m. is not the same as seven a.m. and we can't review every hour of the 666,240 that you have lived. Not to mention we are seeking one moment. Do we have to trawl through the almost 40 million minutes you have experienced?"

"Is it so many?"

"Oh, yes." She leans toward me. "Believe me, Jennifer, among those are a great many you really don't want to relive."

I bite my lip, stifle a cry. As she said those last words a chasm has opened in my mind. Loss, pain, fear... They all wash over me, coalescing into a savage sorrow like a jagged bolt of lightning illuminating all those things I have done in my life and tried so hard to forget, all I have lived through and wished had never happened.

"Have another drink, Jennifer."

My hands are still shaking as I bring the glass to my lips.

Cassis. It is early morning laughter, four friends and the decision to breakfast twice, once on Spanish soil, then a second time in exactly one hour, across a border and a time zone in Portugal. My day when I visited seven a.m. more than once.

"Shall we shortlist that one?"

"Er, it was good fun."

"But not the most fun. All right, try this. I think it's ever so sweet."

Once again I'm on a beach. It's early in the year but the sunrise is warming. Above my head a hundred hot air balloons travel in a stately procession across the cloudless sky. My daughter, five years old, in her favourite yellow wellies, dances, splashing in and out of the shallow pools left by the tide. A wonderful moment. But could I live in it forever?

We go on. The first morning in a new house, the one I had wanted so much. The final one. We never regretted the purchase. A couple of Christmas mornings with the children. Then a surprise. How could I not have realised how good the mornings were with only myself and Paul remaining in the house?

I look at her across the table. "That's it, isn't it? The perfect seven a.m. is one of those when I drink coffee in bed with Paul while we plan our day. I'd like that memory, please."

She nods. "Why not? It's as good as any other. And it has the advantage of not too much detail. It won't take too long for you to get sick of it."

"Get sick of it? It'll be wonderful. It'll make me happy and that's your job, isn't it? Helping me choose my Heaven."

"Whatever gave you that idea, Jennifer? How could endless repetition of one event, however delightful, be any kind of Heaven? No, my dear, my job is to help you select your happiest time so it can be ruined: ultimate boredom accompanied by the pain of losing something so important to you. I did tell you at the start I'm not as high up as an angel. In fact, I have come to claim you for a place a very long way below them.

THE UNKINDNESS OF WITCHES

Could any nightmare have been worse than this?

The crowd of angry faces pressed ever closer. If they were waiting to enjoy my screams, they were going to be disappointed. I would have screamed if I could, but there was a rock in my throat. I had been so sure I could do this; so proud of my courage; so brave, so self sacrificing but now all that was gone. I would have told them the truth if anyone would have listened; I'd have betrayed Cain, told them what he had done and where to find him. But they had a witch to burn. And that had not happened in such a long time.

Nicholas brandished the burning branch over his head. Flames had already devoured its dried up autumn leaves. I had never liked him. We had not been friends and in recent times... Well, I did not want to think about that. I had never imagined him like this though: his face a mask; a rictus grin of pure delight. His was the honour of setting the spark to the tinder around my feet.

All I had to do was burn.

One step towards me, urged on with cheers and yells... one more. I could not breathe. My hands were wet with my own blood. I had writhed my wrists beyond the point of pain. I did not want to burn. I did not want to die. I had done nothing to deserve this. It had not been me.

My eyes closed. I could not keep them open. It was so hot, like the hottest day in summer. Crackling, shouting... but why was I not in agony? I was so afraid. I knew what fire felt like and by now my feet...

Silence.

I forced my eyes open. The flames leapt up; a curtain of red and yellow. Thick smoke billowed. I could no longer see the crowd. But the fire was not touching me; there was a tiny gap between me and the burning wood.

Pressure on my wrists, even the pain from the cuts, was gone. The rope snaked down around my ankles and charred but did not burn. The precarious platform of tangled wood on which I had been perched felt firmer. They had sunk me up to my calves in leaf litter, piling it up with eager hands. Where had it gone? My bare feet were touching stone.

"Hurry up, Hazel. I can't hold this much longer."

Grey granite walls surrounded me. The air was cold. I stared around me. This was unexpected. I had never imagined I would find myself inside a cave when I died.

Three women faced me. They had not been there a moment before.

One of them held out her hand. "Welcome, sister." Was she talking to me? Oh, she was.

"Where am I?"

"Safe, my dear, and for the first time in your life among your own kind."

I doubted that. There was only one kind of creature which could have saved me from dying in the square. These three had to be witches. And I had to get out of there. I wanted to run and fetch help but who would have believed me?

The woman waved her hand in a circular motion and uttered a string of strange words. It must have been some kind of spell, as right away a table and four chairs appeared in the middle of the cave.

"Sit down, my dear. You've a great deal to learn and we don't want to spend the night here. Come along now. Don't be shy. Tell us your name and show us what you can do: what your talent is." She was so pretty for a witch and her voice, oh her voice...

I could not help myself. I sat down.

"There. That's better. Those horrible commoners trying to hurt you like that..." She gave me the sweetest of smiles.

"You're witches. You must be."

"Oh, dearie me. What a crude way to describe us... and yourself too. Don't worry. We know how things have been here. It's natural you've had to hide your true nature but that's all over now. You don't need to be afraid any more. You can show us. Show us everything."

What were they expecting me to do? Why would they...? They could not think because of where they had found me... "You think I'm like you; a witch. Don't you?" I felt my cheeks flush at the shame of it. "Is that the reason you saved me?" My fingers curled round the edge of the chair. What would these creatures do to me when they realised their mistake?

"Relax, my dear. We know you're like us. You can't hide and you no longer have to try. Everything has changed for you now. You're living in a different world, a better world. I am Hazel and my companions are Thaïsa and Laurel. What's your name?"

"Sophie. I'm called Sophie."

"Tell me more, my dear." Despite her soft words her eyes narrowed. Was she becoming annoyed with me?

The one named Thaïsa reached across and before I could stop her... No, I did not want to stop her. I took her hand. There was a warmth in my fingers, a kind of tingling.

Her eyes held mine. "Your powers are well hidden, sister. My touch is not answered. I detect nothing, no energy at all. If I didn't know any better, I would swear we are not the same." Sitting back in a flurry of leaf green silk, which a moment before had been a much deeper, darker shade, and with her eyes changing to match, I had to agree she could not be more right. I was nothing like her. Only the day before I would have been happy to join the crowd in the square to watch a creature like her burn. Now I was less certain. Having your feet buried in kindling and your body tied to a stake ready to be burnt alive does change your views a little. She was still a witch though, and I was sure everyone knew what witches did. Oh, but there was Cain. Yet my brother was different. I knew he was different.

"Sophie, please. Don't force us to be rude and compel you. Show us your talent. You can trust us. After all, we rescued you from burning in the market square. What more proof do you need before you understand the danger has passed? We are your friends."

I could not take any more. Why would I want to talk to these witches? I had to get away and make sure Cain was safe. "Nothing. I can't do anything."

I leapt to my feet and tried to run, to get out of there, to get away from them. They did not move, did not even try to stop me. Reaching the mouth of the cave I stood on a narrow shelf of rock staring out over a wide expanse of mountain peaks. This was not my home.

"Where am I?"

"Does it matter? As long as you are among your own kind what difference does it make where this place is?"

I returned to the chair. "Please take me back. I don't have any magical powers. They made a mistake when they accused me of witchcraft. Sometimes they do, you know."

Hazel pouted. "Don't be ridiculous. If you couldn't do anything, why would they think you could? Besides, we detected the use of power close to your village more than a week ago. Do stop wasting our time. We have saved you. What more proof do you...? Oh, enough!" She reached out and her fingertips brushed my lips. "Tell me!"

I could not stop talking. I told them everything. "It wasn't me. It was my brother. It was Cain. I let our neighbours think it was me so they would leave him alone; so they would burn me and not him." My words of betrayal were mingled with tears.

"Where is your brother now?"

"You'd only hurt him if I told you."

She grasped my wrist and again a gentle warmth spread through me. "We mean what we say. We came here to help. You have done well in trying to protect him but you can't save him, not on your own. But we can. Where is the boy?"

I told them. I described the mill by the race with the small hill behind and the tumbledown cottage next door. In my mind I could see Cain hiding and I told them everything I saw.

Hazel gave me an approving nod. "Good. Now give me some landmark, child. We will go there right away."

Again the words fell from my lips. I had no resistance. I could keep no secrets from these three women. I told them I was afraid of witches and they laughed, the sound merging with the gurgling of the mill stream.

Then the cave was gone...

...and I was standing outside my home.

Thaïsa asked me more questions and I answered them. I told her I had lived there since I was born, first in the miller's house and, after our father died, Cain and I were lodged in a lean-to. We worked all day in the mill for our elder bother, Lucas, even though I was not yet strong enough to heft the heavy sacks of grain on my shoulders and Cain was too young to do anything other than fetch and carry.

He had always performed little tricks: producing feathers and flowers out of thin air and, from time to time, making small pebbles skitter across the floor. Papa would warn him not to let anyone else see, but since our father's death Cain had become reckless. And he would not listen to me. He did more and more of his tricks and they became ever more daring. I was beginning to worry he might be unable to stop. At first he only conjured up little things: cheeses, bread, cakes. I begged him to be careful but still he would not listen. Instead he fetched bigger and bigger objects and that was what had put us in the position which resulted in my being tied to the stake.

We were in the mill and Cain was bored. He wanted be out in the fresh air away from the flying chaff and escaping grain.

Jayne, our sister-in-law, was working on the ground floor with us while our brother fed the hopper on the floor above. She wanted to make us carry the grain sacks, saying, "Yes, I know they're heavy but my husband keeps you, doesn't he? He sees there's food in your bellies and a roof over your heads. What do you do for him? Cain is eight now and you are thirteen. I see no reason why you can't manage one between you."

The next instant we were in the midst of a choking cloud of whirling powder. One of the sacks floated above Jayne's head. It turned a somersault in the air and its contents cascaded over her, settling in a thick carpet round her feet. It was as though she were caught in a mottled brown and grey snowstorm, a blizzard of fine flying flour. She was coated in it.

She screamed at the top of her lungs.

I was frozen to the spot as she fled the mill, a chasing plume of flour trailing in her wake.

From the top of the stairs Lucas gazed down, his mouth gaping open. "What have you done?"

We did not have long to wait for the answer. Jayne was back within minutes, accompanied by a gaggle of neighbours.

I placed myself in front of Cain. I tried to convince them the sack had been on the floor above and had fallen. When I saw they were not going to believe me I told them I had caused the chaos. Lucas, who had seen everything, said nothing. I was dragged away to be tried as a witch but the trial itself was a waste of time: Jayne's vivid account of her ordeal was more than enough to condemn me.

My shoulders slumped as I felt the compulsion to talk dissipate. The witches had heard enough.

I led them to the door of our squalid, one room dwelling. I had no choice other than to trust them.

"Cain, where are you? It's me, Sophie. You're safe."

There was no reply. The room was cold and empty. There was nowhere for him to hide. Had the villagers found him out and taken him away? My heart began to race: I was on the verge of panic.

Thaïsa placed a soothing hand on my shoulder and the fear drained away. "Do not fret, child. There has been no struggle in this room. Nothing is out of place." She trailed her finger through the dust on the surface of our rickety, little table. "No one has been here in days. Now, think, my dear. Where would your brother go if he was afraid and wanted to feel safe?"

"The mill. Yes, to the mill. He might try to hide in there."

"In that case we shall go to the mill."

"What about the crowd in the square? They must have realised by now I haven't been burnt. They could be out looking for me. We could all be in danger. And Cain too."

"There is no danger, girl, not while we are with you. Mere commoners are no threat to us."

We left the house and walked round to the mill door. There was still no one in sight. I wondered whether Lucas had attended the burning, his arm around Jayne as they both witnessed what they thought was my death. I shivered.

Inside the mill all was quiet. I could not even hear the usual scratching from the rats and mice we could never shift even with our three cats. The mill race gurgled but the wheel was held still. No flour was being produced that day.

I climbed the steps up to the grinding platform. Several sacks of grain had been heaped together ready to be emptied into the hopper and begin their journey through the crushing gap between the scalloped channels of the quern stones.

"Sophie! Sophie! You're all right. Oh, Sophie!" Cain raced out from between the sacks, almost sending me flying into the grain shoot. His stick thin arms locked around me. "I was so frightened. I thought you were dead."

"Is this the boy?"

I looked over my brother's shoulder at the witch in the blue dress. "Yes, this is Cain."

He let go of me. His eyes were wide. "Who is this lady? Did she save you?"

"Yes, she did and, Cain, this lady is like you."

Hazel extended her hand towards us and in the centre of her palm appeared a slice of rich chocolate cake frosted with a pale blue icing.

"Are you hungry, Master Cain?"

"Are you a witch?" His eyes became as round as a pair of florins. He was more fascinated than afraid.

"I call myself a sorceress and if your sister has told me the truth, I hope you are going to grow up to be a sorcerer."

He took the cake from her. "I can do things like that." Before I could stop him he was munching into it. "This isn't from Mr. Liffey's bakery, is it? His wife can't make cakes nearly as nice as this."

"No, it wasn't even baked in this country. Now, what can you do, young man? Would you like to show me?"

I wanted to protest but Thaïsa waved her fingers at me and I could not move a muscle. I struggled but neither my body nor my voice would obey me.

Cain had not noticed anything was wrong. He was far too occupied. He opened his hand and there on his palm was Jayne's coin purse, the one which should have been hanging from her belt. "Not bad, eh?"

Hazel chuckled. "Good. That's splendid but the sorcerers to whom we are going to take you will teach you to do so much more. You will be happy with them. They live in a beautiful house on an island in the middle of the river and, if you like, you can eat cake every day. Doesn't that sound wonderful? Come along now. It's time we were on our way." She was about to wave her hand when Thaïsa held up her own to stop her.

"Wait. What about the girl? We must compensate her. You know the rules as well as I do."

"This is an unusual situation. She already has been compensated. We rescued her from the flames. What more could she ask of us?"

Not to be left there like a human statue would have been good.

It was as if Thaïsa knew what I was thinking. "We can't leave her like this. They'll only find her and carry her back to the fire. You're not being fair, Hazel. She may be a commoner but she did risk her life for one of our kind. The young one is her brother and we should be careful if we are not intending to follow custom."

"You're too soft, Thaïsa." Her mouth turned down in a sneer. "You've far too much of a weakness for commoners for my liking. We're not here to watch over them. We have enough to do as it is."

"Perhaps we have, but I still hold we can't reward her service to one of us by letting those fools in the square take her and burn her."

"She can't come with us."

"No, I agree. She can't."

Had Thaïsa lost the argument? Was it true? Was I going to be left there, unable to move, unable even to flee?

Hazel grasped Cain's wrist and he at last began to struggle. "No! I won't go anywhere without Sophie and you can't make me."

The sorceress tutted, twirled her hand and my brother fell senseless to the floor. She waved at me and I was free.

"Thaïsa is quite correct to reprimand me. I will honour your rights. You can have anything you want. A thousand florins is the usual choice."

"Do you expect me to sell my brother to you?"

"No, this is nothing to do with buying and selling. We are obliged to compensate you for the care you have taken of him up to now. You will receive one part right away: a wish if you like. And in the future you may call on us once more. I suggest you hold tight to that promise and use it in your hour of greatest need."

"This is that hour. I don't want your florins. I want you to go back to where you came from and leave my brother and me alone. We will run away together."

She snorted. "Don't be ridiculous. He has to come with us. Now, have you any sensible demands we can meet?"

"You can't give me anything I want. You would have to turn me to stone to make me accept what you are doing. I will follow you wherever you take him. I am determined you will not have him. I will rescue him..."

She touched her fingers together and I saw a faint blue light surround the tips. "That's your last word, is it? You would rather be a statue forever than lose your brother?"

I was so angry I did not see the danger. Not even when she smiled.

"In that case..." Her hand was in the air...

...and we were no longer at the mill. We were in the middle of the village square, now deserted after the burning, the remains of my pyre only embers and ash. No doubt, not realising I had escaped, my neighbours were off, celebrating the success of their afternoon's work.

I felt dizzy, disorientated, close to sleepy.

Hazel looked around her. "What about there?" She was not talking to me.

Thaïsa shrugged. "It's as good a place as any, I suppose, but are you sure this is the right thing to do?"

"You heard her." The witch's fingers ruffled my hair. "She will be so pretty, people will come from far and wide to look at her."

I was standing in the shallow bowl of the village fountain. Around me the square was empty. I could not move my eyes but from their corners I saw my outstretched arms were raised to the height of my shoulders, my hands open and in each one was a smaller stone bowl. I gazed straight ahead. My feet were in the water but there was no discomfort. There was no feeling at all. I knew if I could see myself, I would see the statue of a young girl.

Hazel nodded to herself. "Nice. You will be much admired. Now, farewell."

She was gone. Cain was gone. They were all gone.

Look upon me, friends, and learn of the unkindness of witches. For me not a quick death by fire; instead a slow erosion by weather, wind and water.

Could any nightmare be worse than this?

PERCHANCE TO DREAM

The trains are gone, not even a memory of tracks is left. I won't tell anyone. They'll look at me with eyes full of pity and whisper about insanity. They'll tell me to stop imagining things. It'll be the same as it was with the strawberries. Only this time it might be even worse. I know Greg has had enough. I'm afraid he might leave me.

The night before the strawberries vanished I dreamt of meringue drenched with cream: a dozen ripe berries sandwiched inside, a crown of perfect ripe fruits on top.

"I fancy cooking some sweet treats."

"Does that translate as 'let's drive out to the supermarket?'"

"I'll go on my own if you like."

Greg picked up his keys. "Come on. Lets get it over with."

The fruit aisle was busy as always on Saturday morning. There were raspberries, blueberries, even scattered cartons of blackberries and cranberries, but not a single strawberry, not even a gap where they should have been.

"Damn. I wanted to make strawberry shortcake."

"Is that another new thing you've found on the internet?"

"What do you mean 'new thing'? You love shortcake."

He picked up a punnet of raspberries. "I do and you always make it with these and it's always delicious. Why try to find some new fruit I've never heard of?"

I frowned at him but his eyes didn't crinkle and he didn't start to laugh. Greg could never keep a straight face when he was joking.

Nearby, a man was restocking the bananas.

"Excuse me, do you have any strawberries? I can't see them."

He straightened up and ran fingers through thinning hair. "Can't say I've ever heard of those before. Are they one of those new hybrid fruits?"

We bought the raspberries but I didn't cook shortcake. Instead I opened my book of desserts. There was no mention of strawberries. I was becoming alarmed. I typed "strawberry" into Google but there were no references, just a list of suggestions for words I might have meant.

I didn't know what to do. My memory was clear but it was as if the rest of the world had forgotten.

For hours that night I couldn't sleep. When at last I did I dreamt of candles, tall, white candles on the altar of a church, small scented ones round the edge of a bath in an advert I once saw, bright yellow citronella on a table in Spain. In the morning I tried to find the ones we kept in the bottom drawer. But they were gone.

"What are you looking for?"

"The candles. You know, the ones for emergencies. Have you moved them?"

"No, what do they look like?"

"White, a bundle of six in a box. We've had them years."

"You feeling all right, Pam? Yesterday you were looking for some fruit I've never heard of. Today it's candles and I'm certain I've no idea what they might be."

I couldn't think of an answer. As I made coffee I felt his eyes on me. I could tell he was worried.

By the next morning there were no forks. Greg swore we had only ever had spoons and knives. I overheard him on the phone to a friend, "I think Pam's having some kind of nervous breakdown."

I was scared to close my eyes. But I couldn't stay awake. In the next few days we lost so many things. My dreams were crowded with images: lamp posts, elephants, cheese, cushions and then the trains. I could find no pattern. The losses were random.

Greg tried to reason with me but I was too frightened. He told me to stop babbling. "I've made an appointment for you to see the doctor. She'll know what to do. Perhaps all you need is a few pills."

The pills made me sleepy but more sleep equalled more losses.

I tried placing anonymous posts on social media. "Has anyone else noticed lots of things have gone missing? Does anyone remember strawberries?"

The only replies I got were from cranks who claimed all manner of other things had gone, things I had never heard of. What, for example, was a bird supposed to be?

This morning I don't want to get out of bed. Last night was the most frightening dream yet. Last night I dreamt of Greg.

DOWN IN OUR STORM CELLAR

There's a ghost down in our storm cellar. It moans, screeches, bangs and crashes as it tears round under the house. I'm sure all the anger is because we're invading its home.

I don't want to upset it. Ma says I shouldn't worry because there is no ghost and, even if there were, it wouldn't mind; it'd be pleased to have some company. Besides, where else could we go in storm season, when the easterly winds shake the house and the lightning starts fires in the brushwood and trees round our farm? She says it's safer, but I think I'd rather be out in all that weather than risk being down there with the ghost.

When the sun shines and the winds blow from the west there is no need to go into the cellar so no one does. But Ma and Pa must be afraid because they keep the door locked with a big, old key and a heavy bolt is drawn across it just out of my reach. They pretend it's only dangerous because of the stuff they store: bottles of water, cans of beans and an old camper's stove; things they say I mustn't touch but I know it's all a lie. The real reason is the ghost.

I don't know whose ghost it is. It could be Uncle Percy's. He disappeared soon after I was born. They told me he went out prospecting but never came back. Maybe it's him buried under the uneven flags in the far corner, the darkest part of the cellar, where the lamplight doesn't reach. Or it could belong to Aunt Alice, my mother's sister. Ma says she hasn't heard from her in years. Pa says he's glad. "Good riddance. She were always a bad 'un."

I think he's the bad 'un if he's the one who did her in. She could be in the other corner or bricked up inside the wall. I saw a body in a wall once. It was in a movie. Pa said it was a stupid idea. No one would ever do such a thing in real life. But he would say that, wouldn't he?

I have evidence the cellar is haunted. I read about it in my book. It says right at the beginning, "a cold, clammy atmosphere is a sure sign of an other worldly presence." It's always cold and clammy in the cellar. Sometimes the walls are so damp you can run your hand over them and big, fat drops of water fall from your fingertips. You can see your breath too, at least until Pa lights the oil stove. Then the air is all smoky.

I've decided next time the weather's bad I'm not risking the cellar. I'll run away if they try to make me go in there. I'm already prepared: I've an old blanket folded up in my knapsack; a pack of cookies; a bottle of water and a long torch. I've borrowed one of Pa's big raincoats and stuffed it into the space there was left. They won't notice I've been gone for a while.

When there's a bad storm acomin' they're always so busy. Ma fusses, makes lots of extra food, runs up and down stairs yelling instructions. "Ya never know. We're due fer a twister an' it could take out the dam upriver. We might be trapped for days." She expects me to go sit on the bunk they keep in there, stay outta the way. I don't like the bunk. I'm sure the ghost sleeps there when the door is locked.

Next evening our neighbor rides by the front of the house. "Wanted to warn y'all there's a twister comin' down!"

Ma calls back, "We're ready for whatever nature throws at us. I hope you, Marcie and the boy are as well prepared as we are."

He laughs and waves his whip at me. "See ya after the storm, Mikey. You can come over, spend some time with Gus. He's gotta new pony."

Gus would have. I don't like him but he's the only other boy near my age for miles around so it's see him or see no one.

Ma gives me a push towards the stairs. "Come on. We gotta get the cellar ready. You go down right now and get yersel' comfortable."

I don't think she notices me shiver.

She unlocks the door. The bolt screeches like an animal in pain. Inside is a black hole waiting to swallow me. She lights the lantern kept on a hook high on the damp wall. We don't have any electrics in the cellar. Every year Pa says he's putting them in but he never does.

She's watching so I do as I'm told. I sit on the edge of the damp, rickety old bunk. There's a book on the pillow. It doesn't look very interesting. It's about someone having an adventure flying airplanes. Who cares about that? I would have picked another one about ghosts. I have to learn all I can. Maybe there's a way to drive this one outta the cellar. I can feel it watching me.

"Stay here, Mikey. I'm gonna get the chili off of the stove. I guess we'll be eatin' down here tonight. Hope your Pa gets back soon from seein' to the animals." She leaves me. I hear her feet clopping up the wooden steps.

I run to the door and she's already outta sight. I creep up after her. I will not be alone with the specter. I will not spend another storm in here with it. I have my den in the woods and that's where I'll go. I'm not scared of the wind and a few drops of rain.

Ma has her back to me as I tiptoe through the kitchen. She doesn't hear me because I know which stairs creak on the way to my room.

I drag my knapsack out from inside the wardrobe and hoist it onto my shoulders. I start down the stairs but have to hurry back up as the front door opens.

"All secure, Mary. Time we was in the cellar. Where's Mikey?"

"He's down there already, lookin' at that book you gotten him."

"Oh, good. So no nonsense about it being haunted this time, then?"

"No, I told ya he'd get over it once he stopped readin' them silly stories."

From the top of the stairs, through my part open door, I watch them: Pa carrying the big pan of chili, Ma a handful of plates. I hope they'll be safe from the ghost but I'm not going to chance it.

I have to go quick now, not give them time to realize I'm not in the cellar.

It's so windy, bending the tree tops and making the branches thrash. There's no rain yet but there will be soon enough. The sky is dark as pitch. No stars peep through the fast moving clouds. I'm glad I brought the torch.

I pass the side of the stable. The horses are restless. I can hear them shifting around, whinnying and striking the dirt with their hooves.

There's a noisy whispering from the corn in the field as I squeeze through the gap in the fence, making my way to my secret den. No one knows about this place, not even Gus.

I follow the little trail in the bed of the dried up stream to the biggest tree. I dug out the soil from its roots to make a nice, deep hole. I could be a gopher or anything I like when I pull the low hanging branches down to hide me. This is my place. I rolled in two large, flat rocks, one to sit on, one for a table.

I'm safe here. If no one can find me, the ghost can't either.

I unpack my knapsack and place the cookies and water bottle on the rock beside me. I won't eat yet. I could be here for hours, maybe even 'til tomorrow. I wish I'd brought my book.

It's getting chilly. I pull on my sweater. Without warning, a torrent of cold water pelts down on me through the leaves. I stand up and string the raincoat from the low branches over my head. I've been here in a shower before but this time the coat sags lower and lower. I get a stick and poke it to make the rain run out; it's heavy and sways as though there were a whole lake inside. Then the water is pouring out, straight down one side of the hole. Everything is muddy and the cookies have turned into a scummy soup.

A bolt of lightning fizzes. There's a rumble of thunder in the distance and, as it dies away, I hear a howling in the forest around me. Has the ghost followed me?

I've gotta see. I push the raincoat out the way. It falls into the mud around my feet. I trample on it as I stand up.

"Mikey! Mikey! Where are you?"

No, no! The ghost is pretending to be our neighbor. Through the branches there is something coming towards me. The lightning flashes and everything is so bright. A flapping, white creature spins round in the middle of dancing spears of searing light.

Another rumble of thunder, so loud it shakes the ground and the ghost flees, running off, still hollering my name.

I fall back onto my stone. I don't want to be here anymore. I wanna go home. But that's the direction the ghost took. What if it's out there waiting for me?

The bottom of the den is filling with water. I can't stay here any longer. I begin to climb but the soil turns to liquid mud. It cascades down around me while the raincoat grasps my feet like slippery tentacles, tripping me. I sprawl across the boulders. A swirling whirlpool engulfs me, the torch is swept away on coffee colored waves topped with foam.

"Help! Help!" I shout. I yell. I scream. But the water thrusts me forwards. The dam must have been swept away. The dry bed filling; the deep river reclaiming its original course.

A splash as loud as an explosion. Waves close over my head as the tree crashes down. Branches like long fingers pull at me. A larger bough strikes me. My mouth fills with mud.

I cannot breathe. I cannot breathe.

I'm on dry land. Broken branches strewn around me. I have no idea how I got here. I guess I must have pulled myself out using the tree roots.

I stagger to my feet. The waters surge past me, heading towards the farm. They were once the boundary of our land. I guess they will be again. The fields are flooded, ankle deep, in restless eddies of cold water. The drowned corn stalks sway like reeds in a river.

I stumble through the remains of the fence and there is our farmhouse, all lit up like during the holidays. They must be looking for me.

I begin to run. I don't care what is in the cellar so long as I am there; so long as I am dry; so long as I am safe.

I race down the steps and into the basement. Ma is there but Pa is missing.

Our neighbor's wife sits beside her on the bunk. "They'll find him, Mary. Don't you worry."

"I'm here, Ma. I'm back. Look, I'm safe," I shout. I touch her on the shoulder.

But she doesn't move. She doesn't look at me. She doesn't hear me.

There's a ghost down in our storm cellar. I moan, I screech, I bang and crash as I tear round under the house.

THE BITTER TASTE OF THIS RED

I don't like this one, no sweetness, a child. But why a child?

I wasn't crafted with so much care to be put to such a use. No resistance. Yielding too easily. For me, too cool. The skin a thin layer, the red more bitter than any other I have tasted. Dissenting, unwilling, I buckle. I bend round white, leave untouched crimson, seek the richer, the darker. Not pleasing? Why would I please, when I in my turn am not pleased? When I am in all conscience misused! Where is the battle for which I was forged?

Plunged once again into my darker home, enfolded in another skin long dead, no red though a shadow of flavour remains, I wait.

Bright light and softness; the rasping of tearing fibres; the non taste of clear on my sharp teeth; the last thin wisps of the darker red mingling in streams within and muddying the clear. The dripping of flowing droplets until I am dry and thirsty once more. Now follows the time of honing, of striking, of becoming again my sharpest self; ready to find a sweeter red.

Ah but the next one is also young and bitter. He who wields me cares nothing for my discomfort. Once more I twist but not enough and white grates like the sour cheese insult visited upon me one darkness ago when there was no flesh for them to consume beside the heat. I welcomed the clear, and the cleansing, rasping fibres, as I would welcome them again. Instead there is more bitter red.

Not here for this; not for this was silken metal folded over anvil and into heat, my creator striking with weight great enough to ring louder than thunder. Sparks brighter than day. The song of the hammer beating honesty, beating honour and truth. Not one beat speaking to corruption. No taste given to me for bitter red. My creator giving me into other hands.

"Use this one well, Sir Hugo. It is the best sword I have ever made."

I shone with his pride, with his skill, with his artistry. I will remember who made me and why. I will not fail him. I await my battle.

We leave the place of bitter red, travel over rolling seas, nothing more for me beyond the cleaning and the honing. On land again and for a while all is well with me. There are only clashes in open light, under canopies, observed and cheered. Comparisons made between myself and others. Those who hold us are play fighting, friend on friend, though there is true rivalry between some in this pretence of battle. No red drawn save by accidental wounding, though I discover there are among the crimson streams some of surprising sweetness. Why would there be such corruption here? Were these not the best of knights? Did they not serve the best of kings?

And then within the dark of stone cold passages, the one who wields me speaks untruths and receives them in return. A heavy clinking of coins in a bag beside me, their metal whispering to mine that all is not well. They too are misused. No honest trade, no buying of bread or meat but of a life. They tell me it will be mine to take. I shiver along my length in fear of the taste of more bitter red.

My edge is honed to greater sharpness. There will be no rest tonight. I am held, reflecting firelight, and the deep blue eyes of he who wields me. Had I the power, I would twist within his grasp. I know I would find great sweetness in his veins. I call upon my creator, with his leather apron and the heat of the furnace at his back, but he does not come to me. There is no rescue, no release. I have no will to resist. I am readied and will be misused. I am sheathed and fear the drawing of me.

Up steps and into a high tower, through an arch and into the warmth of a room holding small children. Two boys.

"I won't wake you. I am come to make you sleep forever," he says with laughter in his voice.

I cannot help them. I do as I have no choice other than to do. Their beds and the stones awash with the bitterest, sourest red.

As he prepares to carry me from the place, others arrive. He draws me but I slither from his grasp. I have let the bitter red soak me; let myself become slippery; let myself betray him. But it is not the way of my kind. I know I too must be punished.

Before the bereft king, sword and assassin traitors both, he and I are taken. Held in another knight's strong grasp, bent over his armoured knee, I break; snapping across, falling in shards to lie on stones. Fragmented, I lose myself, hilt and blade gone from each other. We will not meet again. For us there will be no battles.

I am changed, reformed by a hand less skilled. I gain a new hilt, though the pattern hammered into my surface by my original creator remains unaltered. This maker too is pleased with his handiwork.

"This is the finest quality steel. It'll give you years of service. It's the best knife I've ever made."

I do my best to shine, to show off his limited skill, but he is no artist.

His customer spins me on my point. My new hilt is not well balanced and I fall onto the table. "Maybe the metal is good but you're asking too much."

The maker shuffles his feet and reduces his price, sells me for less than I would have cost to make had he purchased my metal instead of finding it on the ground outside the castle, thrown out as tainted.

My new life begins. It suits me better than slitting the throats of innocent infants. The meat, already cold when I touch it, has no taste. But I am, after a fashion, content to be useful.

The butcher cuts himself: he has taken no care of me, not honed me enough. My dulled edge, more deadly than a sharp one, skitters over flesh, slices deep through skin and into such sweetness as I have never known. Even my traitor knight would not have had such flavour.

He curses and throws me across the room. I shudder into the fragile timbers of the door. I do not care for the taste of old, sapless wood. He leaves me there.

Later, in the darkness, a woman with a pale lantern and face of purple bruises comes into the room. She hasn't much strength but she wrests me from my prison. "You hurt him today. Can you do so again?"

I am surprised she speaks to me. Only my creator has ever done so before. There is warmth in her voice and behind it something else. She wraps me in cloth and places me inside her pocket. I sense her purpose.

Again I take a sleeping life and at last it is a guilty one; the sweetest red flows over me. I do not know his corruption but I taste the depths of it.

The woman draws me from him. I am reluctant but have no choice other than to go. She takes me out into the night. Are we to leave together? I would serve her. I would fight for...

Flung from her hand, I am in the air. Deepest clear, though filled with mud, clasps me to it. I sink and there are fish between me and the woman.

And she is gone.

I lie in mud. There is nothing to taste, nothing to see. The hilt placed on me by the second maker becomes loose and in time we are separate. How long until I am discovered again?

Caught in a net, held in a hand in the light, the last of the mud and clear dripping from me.

"What's that?"

"It's a bit of an old blade."

"Throw it back."

"No, it's still shiny and it's got a pattern down it."

I am passed from hand to hand. Two boys so similar to the ones in the tower.

"We could take it to the museum. The curator will know how old it is."

I am carried aloft as though I were a trophy. Rubbed with some strange fabric, not wool but soft and warm, young fingers trace the lines still etched deep into my surface by my creator. We enter a building and there is another woman. She also holds me to the light. She breathes on me and I taste her excitement.

"This is wonderful: a rare treasure. And I know I've seen something like these markings before. Come along." She leads the way to another room. "These are the belongings of a medieval knight who held a manor near here. He was beheaded as a traitor but his son rescued his armour and his descendants held on to it until the last of them gave it to us. Just look at this. The blade you've found has the same design as this fragment of his sword. It could even be the missing part. I'm sure, once our preservation people have finished their job, we'll be able to add it to the display. The two pieces do look as though they belong together. Perhaps the sword was broken in battle."

Oh, thank you, my creator. Reunited, I will be part of the best display. Shining, I will show your skill and artistry. I will remember who made me and why. No more bitter red for, though I never fought, my battle now is over.

MY HOME IS A PLACE OF COMPLETE PERFECTION

I have drawn the curtains. All the doors are locked. I run my fingers over the neat stack of silver blister packs on the bedside table to my left. I smile as I pop out the contents of the first one. The pills fall, hard bright, sugar coated but bitter within, ripe with the promise of oblivion. All I need now is enough time before anyone comes looking for me. Before they break down the door.

The room is silent. Once there was a clock that ticked, disturbing my thoughts, but I removed it, burying it beneath the other rubbish in the bin. Now there is nothing left to distract the mind or the eye; no pictures, not even of the children. When Richard moved out I painted the walls an unblemished cream and laid a carpet of the same colour, artfully matched, trimmed with care to blend in seamlessly. I am enclosed in a pale cocoon, only a little light filtering through the floor length drapes.

All is prepared. I count the pills. I know how many I will need, how many it will take. And I have more than enough.

Sweetness on my tongue, a small sip from the tall glass and I am ready for the next one.

I have done this so often, each time with an increased dose. I must control my descent into the coma as a diver does when emerging from the depths. The techniques I have practised for so long must not fail me now. Not when I am so close.

My eyelids flutter, an unexpected physical sensation. Did it happen last time and I forgot or is this something new?

What does it matter? The die is cast.

I will indulge my memory for a short while. I am confident of my ability to regain control as the pills take effect.

Dr. Marshall was the first one to take me seriously. My family called me lazy because I preferred to stay in bed rather than suffer the unpredictability of those around me. I loved my dreams, even though in those early days they were random slices of Heaven. When I enrolled in his research programme he began to teach me how to control my night visions; "lucid dreaming", he called it.

"Here, Sarah, try these." He handed me two white pills. "They will extend and deepen your sleep. Don't worry. There are no side effects."

That night was the first time I saw the house. It was isolated, at the end of a winding country road, flowers in the garden, a drystone wall separating it from a wild meadow. Beyond this, though I could not catch a glimpse of it, I knew was the sea. This place had nothing in common with our cramped third floor flat in the city tower block.

For a while there was only the house but my ability was developing. I discovered if anything appeared out of place, I could remove it, will it away and the next time I dreamed it would be gone, replaced with something more like perfection.

A few more sessions and the family began to appear. Richard... but not Richard. This version was all romance, all care, all love. The new baby was a smiling, cooing darling, with a cloud of midnight hair and deep brown eyes. Her sister never threw a tantrum, never disrupted. But, even so, one day I realised I didn't want them any more. They were nothing more than intruders. So I erased them and it was as though they had never existed.

I hated every moment when I was awake, the daytime Richard and I rowed over every little thing. Why could he not be more like the lover in my other world? I had ceased to think of it as only dreaming. It was as real as any other place I had ever been, only better, so much better.

"Wake up, Sarah. Don't you see this is getting out of control?" He grasped my shoulders and shook me.

I stared at him, a stranger, not my Richard, not the man who walked hand in hand with me down to the bay.

"Go away. I don't want you here."

I was so pleased when he did leave and took his noisy girls with him. My nights were now my own, two a week spent at the centre and for the remainder I had my little white pills.

For a while nothing changed, though, because I called in sick so often, I was in danger of losing my job. But more important to me was the fact I now needed more pills than Dr. Marshall was willing to prescribe. I had to find a solution. I couldn't bear to be away from my home.

One evening I managed to take a carton from the trolley while the researcher was distracted. I hugged them to me. They would last me at least a month.

I had thought Dr. Marshall was my friend, my great ally, but a few weeks later, when I arrived at the centre, I found another woman lying in the bed within the cubicle which had been mine for so long.

"What's going on? Who's she?" I felt panic rising in me, my chest tightening, my fists clenching.

"Calm down, Sarah. We need to have a little talk."

"Later. I'm really tired. I'm certain tonight will be a good session."

He shook his head. "No more sessions. I'm afraid you're becoming addicted. Your husband is very worried and, frankly, after listening to what he has to say, so am I."

"There's nothing wrong with me."

"Probably not but I'd rather be safe than sorry. I believe you are starting to confuse reality with your dream state. You must go home. I'll have a word with your GP. He can prescribe something to help you over this. It's for the best. We must act before you become completely dependant on the drugs we give you here."

I could not believe this. Why was he was trapping me in this drab, unhappy place when I ached to be in my garden? I wanted the strong walls of my house around me.

Somehow I stumbled out of the building. In the car I grasped the steering wheel, my knuckles turning white as the tears flowed down my cheeks. I had to have my pills. I had to return to my house. I could not become a refugee trapped in a world I no longer recognised.

There was only one thing I could do. Every unwilling exile has the right to fight to get back to their home.

I waited all night until Dr. Marshall appeared. He was, as always, the last person to leave the clinic. He sauntered across the car park, not a care in the world. I was still accelerating when I ran over him.

His briefcase was thrown clear and I tugged it open. I almost yelled with relief when I found two whole cartons of the precious white pills.

I dragged him into a dark corner by the far hedge then sped to the flat and raced to my room. I peeled off the stained jeans and sweatshirt and threw them down the stairs. My nightgown was thin and cool, similar in design to the floaty pastel dresses I wore at home.

Page 143

The packs are empty. I can feel the drowsiness seeping into my veins. I can't wait to walk up the path into my white house. At the clinic I was warned too many of these pills might well result in a permanent coma. Did they not realise the words were not a threat at all? They were a promise. The nurses whispered in hushed tones about their fears of such a disastrous outcome. I can't understand why, for if all goes well, I will escape from this place. I will live in my white house forever. And why would I not want to be there?

My home is a place of complete perfection.

SHADOW PLACE

With my restless flurry, my flowing symphony of secrets, I divide the land. By day the people come. It is hard for them not to remember, shading their eyes as they gaze across at the unrelenting, ever shifting mudflats. They think too much of the bodies of their heroes and villains, though not a trace remains of the long ago battle. Some fools talk of a lullaby they imagine. But it is only wind blowing over dry reeds and the current drifting through bones of old, fleshless fingers.

Beyond dusk few visitors remain. Those who do, think to spend a quiet night in a small boat rocked to sleep. What makes them believe I will hold their cradle secure in my arms of liquid lies? Though sometimes I do, more often what remains is an empty boat borne on the ripples of a fading wave.

With the dawn I rise, a slight swell from a faraway tide. Diamonds scatter from restless oars while, around the bowed heads of the busy fisherfolk, jewel bright blue, purple and jet black iridescent wings take to the skies. The flies welcome my gifts. Their bloated bodies are swollen from an excess of carrion because in the dark a wolf came to drink. The bank did not hold under his scrabbling paws. He became one more blaze of bleached bones, betrayed by the current and given back to the clear eyed, cruel beaked, cold clawed crows.

Nothing changed for a long time. I was content until she came.

She arrived on a winter's day when my waters were amber, sugar encrusted; a trap just like jam in a jar set for wasps. Her coat was as thin as my own, the child beside her little more substantial than the wing of a dragonfly. She gathered an armful of rushes, white tipped, sharp as unused spears. She sang in a high wisp of a voice; a dream of spring; a time too far off; on the other side of a long, cold season.

Her child, having heard it all before, was not listening.

The reeds rustling, the woman's mind filled with the warmth of the blaze she would make of them once she had returned to her home.

Bored, the child allowed me to lure her eager feet. A moment's hesitation, taking in the pristine, untouched glistening white expanse between her and the further bank... She placed her feet upon me, no blades, no skates, only the thin sheen of worn leather, bound in place with a taut, fish-gut string. She stepped forward thinking my surface iron hard: not snail-shell fragile, to collapse and crunch under the lightest touch.

I remembered her now; on warm days past, a small and slender five, one of a group who threw stones and watched the ripples spread. They mocked me with their youth and careless disregard for what I was. They laughed as in my summer weakness, my shallow time, I could not hold onto them.

I waited for one more brave, one less wary, to leave the game, go far enough from the others but it did not happen.

This girl came the closest, diving down to steal treasure I had hoarded; smooth, round pebbles for so long sifted and churned until to me most precious. Shaking droplets from her brow, she had laughed as she threw them, drying out, losing their beauty, into the arms of her comrades. There, on my bank, so close but beyond my reach, they piled them.

All but one. My favourite. A singular, shining crystal. It resisted polishing, needing none, clear as I am myself on a day of blue sky. She had held it; taken it away from me.

Come autumn, the rains fell. The land cried and filled me to my depth. I took back my pretties before the earth could dry around them again, tugged them free from the roots of persistent blackthorn and wild strawberry, tossed them clean of the clinging mud and created for them a safer store... but my most lovely one was not among them.

The girl slips, slides, glides over my smooth skin. Her coat gapes open and the breeze disturbs the neck of her dress. There, a flash of blue against the dull fabric. My pretty is returning to me. There will be no error this time. She has no comrades close by her now, save her mother, who turns and hesitates in her song. She drops the reeds and cries out to her child.

Why should I listen? Why would I return this one and not the two I took the other day? They had more right. Innocents, they had taken nothing from me.

The child hears her mother's call, responds with an arrogant shout of delight, unaware of the danger. She does not believe there is any reason to be alarmed. I thicken my skin beneath her feet. I want her to come closer to my deepest channel.

The woman holds out a branch, leans from the shore. She is too wise to trust me... but she cannot reach.

The girl leaps, her pirouette taking her ever nearer to my middle. I shift my currents. I am ready.

No more waiting, a trap prepared and sprung... A long shiver, a short splash and all will be over.

The mother need not weep. In spring I will return her treasure as mine will have been returned to me. I will give this girl a crown of marsh marigolds, enfold slippery, fresh weed among the strands of her hair, wrap her in a winding sheet of pale pink lilies and dark green leaves.

I cannot allow her to be buried. But she will still wear my stone. So, before her mother's grasping fingers can close on anything as substantial as bone, I will twist the girl in my strongest eddies and raise her small hand in final farewell.

What is the woman doing? What are these words carried to me on the wind? She holds up her clenched fist, from which a string of bright droplets are now suspended. More pretties, so similar to the singular one her daughter wears.

Can it be she thinks to offer me a bargain? I have never made one before. I have sometimes been capricious; on a whim allowed a struggling salmon to escape from a strong net, a fisherman to regain his footing among my shifting, treacherous slime. This is different; a choice!

The woman lowers the jewels. On her knees now, the shining strands caress my surface. They catch and scratch a faint pattern, cut into me a little path which leads nowhere as she swings them out of my reach again.

I want to take her, place her beside her daughter but she is too clever. With her other hand she keeps a tight hold on the branch of the overhanging willow and she has fastened her belt around its slender trunk.

The willow arcs, the farthest tip of its outermost branch within reach of the girl. No friend of mine, this tree, thrusting its sturdy roots into me to drink, even when I have little to give. When it first sprouted I tried for three seasons in a row to dislodge it with fierce floods but it clung on and now it is anchored too deep.

The girl remains motionless. The willow branch taps her hand as her mother continues to offer me the bait. The weak winter sun conspires with them both. No droplets of my waters ever sparkled so, six rays of light captured on a slender thread of gold. For a moment I am distracted.

Now the child is clinging to the willow branch. Her heels skitter as she is dragged across me. No! I refuse to let her go. Beneath her body my surface forms a thousand sudden cracks, the sound like a hunter's gun in the cold silence, startling the sleeping crows who, wings flapping, take to the air. For an instant they form a dark cloud hiding the sun, concealing the light from the gilded string, turning the jewels to mere, dull pebbles.

Though I am now liquid, my solid form lost except where ripples still carry a white sheen, though I send the strongest waves to try and drag down the heavy folds of the coat and dress which clothe the child, still I am no match for the woman and the willow. I am too slow, the child becoming a wet and slippery catch no longer within my bounds.

The mother does not have to keep her bargain. Indeed I do not expect her to yet, with an overarm throw, the jewellery tumbles and splashes between the floating, jagged slivers, all that remains of frozen water. They sink down into my secret depths. Too late I realise I would have preferred to keep the girl.

I console myself. This would only have been one more drowned child. There will be a thousand others. Maybe more skaters will come before this day is over. A bargain once made can be recognised and resisted if it is offered again.

I can wait. I am not in a hurry. It does not even have to be a child. There are others who are not so wise. See how smooth, how inviting my waters are as they lap around your feet.

What about a little moonlight dip?

Are you sure I can't tempt you?

THE RAT SQUID OF CALAMARIS

They regard me with dull eyes. They have no interest in what I have to say. I cannot make them understand. It's too late. As far as they are concerned my story is over. I have been judged and found guilty. Here on this beach, tied to a stake, gazing out over the crashing waves, I see no hope of escape.

It's all my own fault. I should have abandoned my cousin, Carl, when I realised what he was going to do. But I didn't, even though I could hear in my head my grandfather telling me, "You're a fool, my girl. Get out of there. Leave him to it." Yet this destiny is as much my grandfather's fault as anyone's. I and those who preceded me only followed his lead.

I was brought up to show respect for the family and to keep the source of our vast and ever increasing wealth a closely guarded secret. As a child the bedtime stories my mother and father told me were of strange creatures who dwelt in the depths beneath our island home. Not until my seventeenth birthday did I discover those tales were not mere invention. Instead, they had been a kind of preparation, intended to help me understand the unbelievable truth: my family straddled two worlds and made money out of both.

There are caverns hidden between the jagged rocks of the cliffs which overlook the bay and one of them holds the entrance to a tunnel: a long, vertical shaft of igneous rock descending from light shadow into pitch darkness. My grandfather had fallen down it while playing hide and seek with his sisters. Like Alice down her rabbit hole, he tumbled a hundred feet or maybe more and landed, as she had, on a bed of soft sand surrounded by a myriad of shallow pools.

Surprised to be alive, he staggered to his feet and, at the tender age of fifteen, discovered the key to riches beyond measure.

He followed a long passage toward a distant light. After ten minutes or so he emerged from the mouth of another cave. Outside, stretched across a beach of silver sand was a hazy vision: a mirage of mismatched structures; some of wood, some of stone and a few of blocks cut from the sand itself; a small, twisted tangle of dwellings under a blazing sun as hot as ours is at midday in the desert.

Through the shifting heat he made out creatures, much shorter and rounder than any human race, with a green hue to their skins and hair, but with arms, legs and heads similar to ours. In his diary he wrote, "I felt like Gulliver." Hiding among a jumble of rocks by the tunnel entrance he observed for a while as a stream of them entered a large structure on the edge of the settlement. Some carried covered burdens in their arms; others dragged packages on small trolleys behind them. When they came out again the burdens were gone and the trolleys were empty.

After a while, as dusk fell, the strange people ceased visiting the building. There came a low sound like a huge gong and at once all of the creatures made for another structure over on the far side of what he had by now decided must be a village. Within a few moments all activity had ceased and the beach was empty.

Unable to contain his curiosity any longer, he crept over to the deserted building. Opening an old, wooden door covered in carved snakes he found himself in a wide open space. A handful of tall candles burned in sconces attached to the plaster walls, down which tallow had dripped, and in their flickering light he saw abstract paintings of every size as well as rough hewn sculptures made of dark wood and pale stone. Unsure how long he could risk remaining, he had to force himself to tear his eyes from the curious artefacts. Was this some kind of art gallery? There was no sign of anything resembling price tags and many of the works lay rolled onto their side on the sandy floor. Some were even scuffed where they had been trodden upon.

That day he stole three of the smallest pieces.

None of the creatures challenged him as he left the village. He didn't think any of them had seen him as the central square was still deserted. He retraced his steps to the tunnel entrance and only then did he wonder how he would get out of this strange world. He had no skill in climbing and his original fall had been close to vertical.

He need not have worried however. He later learned one of his sisters had seen him enter the cave and alerted the family.

He heard his father's voice echo eerily down the stone shaft. "Richard, can you hear me, my boy? Are you all right?"

"Yes, I'm fine, not hurt at all. Can you get me out?"

They managed to obtain a long rope ladder which belonged to a neighbour who happened to be a caver and, after a bit of a struggle, Grandpa Richard was once again back in his own world.

His parents would not believe his wild story until they set eyes on the three small statues. The subjects of two of them unmistakeably people and, as they were made from plain white wood and there was no scale to judge them by, Richard's father laughed at the suggestion they were not at all like us. The third however was a

Page 153

different matter. It depicted some kind of animal, rather like a hybrid of a rat and a squid. Anyone who saw it could not help feeling uncomfortable. The eyes might only be painted stone but they glared out in a strange, malevolent manner and were so placed they followed you as you moved around. It was as though the stone creature were contemplating an attack. My grandfather once said to me, "It felt as though the beast was some kind of predator and I its prey. Had I seen the statue in the clear light of day, I would never have touched it." He was tempted to take it back but the impulse did not last long.

By contrast, his father was fascinated and, as he had never seen anything like it before, he decided to try to sell it. He argued there was sure to be a market for anything so unique and bizarre. And he was soon proved right.

After some discussion the family decided to claim it was Richard himself who had sculpted the beast. At auction it sold for more money than the family could have made in five years. Richard became famous overnight and the pressure mounted on for him to come up with more of the intriguing statuettes.

The next time he descended the shaft he did not go alone. His father and uncle accompanied him. From the world with its odd, little village and its sun drenched beach they brought back a sackful of similar misshapen horrors.

And so the crime spree began.

At first my family were careful not to encroach upon this strange place too often, deciding to climb down the ladder only once or twice a year. But it was difficult to contain their greed.

Because so many of the strange statues resembled hybrids of squids mixed with elements of other creatures, they named the world they had found "Calamaris".

As time went on, the slow moving inhabitants made no effort to stop the pillaging humans. Perhaps the unceasing heat of their sun made them languid as they idled through their long, hot summer. The only hint of resistance came when my grandfather's uncle travelled further into the village but, as the natives had nothing more lethal than short knives with which to threaten him, he ignored them. On entering a couple of the dwellings he was disappointed to discover no further artworks, only rough furniture and crude pottery. It was clear the only things worth taking were in the building where the statues were stored.

And so, after many years, came my own turn to descend to our treasure world. My first two trips were uneventful; the natives kept well away from our party, only observing from a distance with their hooded, green eyes.

Before my third trip I said to my parents, "You do know what we're doing isn't right, don't you? Why haven't we considered trading with these people rather than just stealing from them?"

"We did try once," my father replied. "We took them some nice, shiny objects but they wouldn't even look at them. We tried books, clothes, even cheese but it was no use. They're too dim, these strange people. They only thing they can do well is sculpt."

"They've got good imaginations though, haven't they?" The first time I had seen one of the carved rat-squids it had given me nightmares for months and I still found them unnerving years later.

"Maybe they have. I suppose it's like dragons in our world, nothing more than mythology and fairy tales."

By then our family had been visiting and pillaging the other world for almost sixty years. In all that time we had never seen a trace of any living thing as weird as the hybrid creatures carved in wood or in stone.

True, none of the few animals, birds or fish we did see in that place was exactly the same as at home but they were not all that dissimilar.

I nodded in agreement with my father's words, though as I did so a cold wind stirred the sand and ruffled the green hair of the nearest natives.

Members of the family were by this stage raiding the alternate world on an almost weekly basis. What else could we do? We had customers to please, orders to fulfil, a never ending waiting list for the rat-squid statues.

One day my father suggested my cousin, Carl, and I were old enough not to require supervision. Besides, he said, he was no longer as spry as he had been and climbing the rope ladder was getting a little difficult for him. He had considered replacing it with a more permanent construction but did not want anyone else to stumble upon it and discover our secret. So Carl and I became the next generation of thieves to raid the village inhabited by those strange creatures.

We would each carry on our backs a substantial rucksack in which to collect our stolen booty. I always hoped we might find one of the larger artworks: those fetched more than ten times as much as the others.

But on this, the last visit, once inside the building a shock awaited us. We found the floor strewn with large splinters of wood and smashed fragments of stone. There wasn't an intact carving in the place.

Carl swore under his breath. He struck the wall with his fist. "They've moved everything out. So they think they can hide our stuff from us, do they?" He pulled a gun from his pocket. "This'll make them show me where they've taken it all." He strode through the door.

I was at his heels. "Wait, Carl. We don't want to hurt them."

"Why not? They're little better than animals."

I couldn't stop him. He broke into the nearest dwelling and yelled at the occupants, "Where are the statues?"

They did not react. It was as though he were not there. They continued to ignore him even when he shot one of them.

I felt sick. How could these creatures understand us? In the six decades since we had discovered their world, not one member of my family had made any attempt to communicate with them, except by leaving trinkets, which the inhabitants never touched. They had let us steal their sculptures as though the objects meant nothing to them.

As I stood in the doorway, shocked by Carl's actions, the unmistakeable reverberating clang of the village gong reached my ears. At once the four remaining occupants of the dwelling became animated. Silent but determined, they pushed past me.

Carl watched with his mouth agape as they trooped out to join their fellow creatures. In a long line they snaked their way across the sand towards the large building on the opposite edge of the settlement.

"Come on, cuz!" Carl thrust me aside and raced after them.

"What are you going to do? Kill a few more? You haven't enough bullets for that. Look how many of them there are." I had never seen more than perhaps twelve or thirteen natives together, but now so many were engaged in their relentless march through the open doors I could not even count them.

"I'll bet that's where they've taken our stuff." Carl was ahead of me but I managed to grab his arm.

"If they have, they're not going to just give it to us this time. We'll have to use our brains if we want any more statues."

He stopped. "What's that supposed to mean?"

"We wait. We know they only stay in that building for a short while then they all go home again."

"Yeah, you're right. We could sneak in after their meeting, see if there's anything worth taking."

He led the way back to the tunnel and there we stayed until the daylight had dwindled away. We switched on the torches we always carried, the ones we used when walking between the shaft and the beach.

Beyond the cave entrance all was quiet. At the heart of the settlement, doors were closed and windows shuttered. A clear path was open to us. It struck me we were fortunate there were no guard dogs in this world. In fact there were few animals of any kind: no cats and not many birds either, which was strange when there were no obvious predators around.

We arrived at the building. I half expected there to be guards but instead the doors were not even locked.

We stepped into a warm interior filled with the whisper of softly falling water. Our torches were not necessary as fires burned in braziers at intervals around the walls. The flickering light illuminated a set of steps leading down into a tiered area, like a miniature amphitheatre. In the centre a fountain played and surrounding it were many sculptures of the rat-squid. But these were so different to the ones we had taken. It was like comparing Michelangelo's David to the first attempts at sculpture by a talentless amateur. Hideous in their beauty, they both mesmerised and terrified me at the same time.

And in that moment I understood everything. This was not a meeting room; it was a temple. I saw now why the natives had not stopped us taking the other statues. Why would they? Those we had stolen had been their discards, work they regarded to be of such inferior quality it was not worth exhibiting them, let alone giving them a place in the temple among all this ugly perfection. We had been doing nothing more than helping ourselves to their rubbish: dustbin men from another world. Perhaps we had even been performing a useful service for them. No one likes destroying a religious icon, even when it is inferior dross.

"Wow!" I had forgotten Carl. He leapt down the steps and crept round the statues, peering at each one. "This is it, the real deal! Think what these'll fetch."

"No, we can't take them. Don't you see...?"

He was already stuffing one of the smaller objects into his rucksack.

"Put it back!"

He sneered at me. "No way. Now, you pick one of them up as well. We have to get a move on."

"No!" I stood my ground.

I don't think I believed it when he pointed the gun at me. "I said pick one up." He gestured with the pistol.

It went off. Maybe it was an accident but the noise, a reverberation like thunder, cut through the peace of the place. The bullet must have hit the gong, since shimmering waves of vibrations echoed round the walls.

"Come on. Let's go." Even he had the sense to know we were in danger.

We raced out of the door and skidded across the sand. It was the wrong direction for the tunnel but the settlement lay between us and safety and we didn't dare go that way.

With unaccustomed speed, a horde of natives streamed towards us. In a moment we would be overcome.

Carl had the gun in his hand again, though I knew it was a waste of time.

But the creatures never reached us. Instead they all entered the temple building.

"Idiots!" Carl stood panting. "See. They don't care. We can take this." He shook the rucksack at me. "And tomorrow we can bring some equipment, take one of the larger..." He broke off as a long, low wailing reached our ears, a plaintive howl mixed with so much fury.

They had discovered their loss.

Somehow we made it to the tunnel. Carl was ahead of me. He was a little older, a lot stronger and much more athletic, so a faster climber. Besides, I made the mistake of looking back into the tunnel.

The nearest pursuers were mere seconds behind us. I laid my hand on the rope ladder, pulled myself as high as I could. My foot was on the fifth rung...

...when I fell to the ground, the ladder coiling around me.

From up above I heard Carl call out, "Sorry, cuz." I guess he had not wanted to take the risk of the creatures following him into our world, so to save himself he had cut the rope.

He was gone. He had deserted me. He had abandoned me to the creatures.

Three days have passed. I understand a little of what they say. I am declared a blasphemer, an outsider who has sullied their temple; insulted their god.

But it took me until this moment to also realise the god they worship is a real, living being. No imagination was required to design the statues for now before me, emerging from the breakers, with piercing eyes and huge, wide open maw, shaking foam from a writhing nest of ghastly, white tentacles...

ROMANCE IN A TIME OF DYSTOPIA

I am alone again.

As I wake, my memories of how I got to this place are the usual messy jumble. Did they allow us to spend the night together? Or did it all come to an end long before I climbed the crumbling stairs, got into the creaking glass lift or used whatever other route it was that led here?

It's a small room. I'm lying in a single bed, mounded into the centre to avoid broken springs. The floor is covered by a faded carpet. There's a wardrobe with a broken door and a table with more scratches than surface. No viewscreen, unless it's built into the wall and disguised as stained, peeling flock wallpaper. There is no mirror so I can't check my appearance. Not that I want to.

"Come on, Gina. It's another day in paradise!" I joke with myself but not even I find the words funny.

I swing my legs out of the bed. The tattered, grey blankets smell musty, though it could be I need a shower. Risky things, showers. I've known them rain ice or just the opposite.

My feet tangle in a pile of clothes. I don't bother to examine them. One time they were crawling with lice, another spattered with someone else's dried blood. It's best not look too closely. I have to wear something. I can't leave this place in a thin, patched cotton nightdress.

As I pull the gown over my head, I discover this time they have not taken everything from me. A wave of relief passes through me. I have not lost my present for Michael.

There are objects on the table: a carafe of water, a glass and a book with no cover, the title scratched out. I'm supposed to open it and discover if it's a guide to what lies beyond the door.

Instead, I take a long gulp straight from the carafe. The water is brackish, warm and just a little stale but it's better than nothing.

I pick up the book and throw it onto the bed. "I'm not going to read it!" I hope I sound defiant. It's a small decision and I doubt if it will make any difference, but at least I am making a choice. I have to keep up the pretence to myself that I still possess some tiny fragment of free will.

I open the door and beyond is a white walled passage with a tiled floor. A hospital perhaps? There's a room a little way along with a plate in old fashioned lettering saying, "Bathroom".

I enter and inside I find everything I need, including a ragged, grey towel. Still no mirrors or windows but there is a shelf. And on it is the same book or maybe an identical copy. Who knows?

"Still not going to read it!"

As I leave I slam the door behind me. It takes a while for the echoes to die away.

Out in the corridor, I choose my direction, not back toward the room but round a corner. There is a set of stairs, wide enough for three people. This is an enormous building. I can't hear any voices but I'm certain I won't be alone. That's not the way it works. Somewhere, perhaps not too far away, is Michael and he will be searching for me just as desperately as I am for him. If only we didn't care so much about each other, this might be easier. But, then again, I have no proof of that. Perhaps I never will have.

I don't remember when Michael and I met or even if we had a life together before all this began. We might have been married. There could be children in our past. But all that is gone now, hidden behind an impenetrable wall of shifting, imprecise impressions. It's as though someone took a rusty old knife and cut away part of my mind. A knife, yes, not a scalpel. That would have made a clean incision, left no ragged threads to torment me with glimpses of what might once have been; all our possible history drowned by a kaleidoscope of sharp and bitter memories.

I do not trust those memories. I do not trust anything or anyone.

Except Michael.

I love Michael and he loves me. This is my rock, the only stable truth I can cling to in this whole contorted universe. It is the reason I am bringing this present to him.

I have reached the foot of the staircase. Ahead is an empty atrium. There are dead trees languishing in pots, groups of grubby chairs round tables covered in dust. Michael is not here. I will have to venture outside if I am going to find him. And I must find him.

By the door is a desk. I have to pass beside it. The book is there again.

I sigh as I reach for it. I might as well open it. I have finished with making my futile stand for the time being.

There is no cover, no title page. Before me is a picture and a one word caption, "Crime". In the black and white drawing a woman and a man stand over a third figure and I have no doubt that one is dead. I have no doubt he has been robbed. I have no doubt I have seen him before. Could he be Michael? Is my love already beyond me? Have we had our last meeting?

The book falls from my hand, pages fluttering like the wings of a dying bird.

I walk through the door.

Outside, a cold wind blows along the empty street of a post apocalyptic world. There are no planes overhead and the bombs which created the destruction around me did not fall in the recent past. A thick, grey dust covers everything. It drifts round hollowed out ruins, across broken walls like scattered stone teeth. I can feel it settling on my face, see it coating my clothes. Is this the one where I die of radiation sickness? Or is it something else? Is it a portent of what is to come or a memory of what has passed?

I close my hands over the present I have for Michael.

"What are you doing, woman? Get out of there!" The shout comes from behind me.

I turn. A man in ragged clothes is eyeing me. Now he beckons. I do not think it is Michael but I walk over to him anyway.

"Don't you know it'll be night soon and the walkers will be on the prowl?"

"Yes, I suppose they will."

He stares harder at me. As usual my lack of knowledge confuses someone local to this place.

"Come on. I'll take you to the shelter. You can explain yourself when we're safe."

I don't bother to ask what we will be safe from. I have experienced too many threats. I don't care any more. But I go with him. I have found Michael in shelters before.

This one is a basement. Its wraithlike, shadow-thin occupants shiver. There is no electricity here, no running water except that which trickles down the damp walls. These are not survivors. Or at least they won't be survivors for much longer. Many are hairless and all are sick, displaying

Page 164

multiple lesions on greying limbs. No outside threat is required to end this colony.

I look around, make my necessary checks, while keeping my present for Michael concealed.

He is not here. Time to go.

They watch me with tired, listless eyes as I abandon them.

Back on the street dusk has fallen and the ruins all around me are alive with muffled squeaks and the skittering of claws. Every city has its vermin. Sometimes I have the strange and fleeting thought that Michael and I belong with them.

For the next three days I wander through the dead and dying landscape. I find water in broken pipes. There must have been rain not long ago. Does the liquid have a strange taste or is it my imagination? It has to be contaminated, as does the food I find in one of the ruins, a half dozen tins with no labels, the contents a bland substance that might be some kind of vegetable stew. I am becoming weak. I keep being sick. There are open sores on my legs.

I must find Michael soon.

Another day, another ruin to search.

"Gina! Oh, Gina!"

I hear the call and try to run. I have so little strength, but it is enough. I fall into his arms.

"Michael!"

"Oh, my darling, come away with me." He takes my hand and, as we walk together arms entwined, the city fades into nothingness; our love once again allowed its brief existence.

I say to him, "Let's pretend none of this is real. Let's imagine we are in a garden, on a path under trees, surrounded by flowers and with the sun shining down on us. Let's be one more couple romancing on a summer's day. Close your eyes, Michael, and let me kiss you."

It is time to give him my present.

I draw the long, sharp blade from beneath my dress, pull back my arm and stab upwards with all the strength and love I possess.

I feel the sharpest pain and I watch our blood mingle. I was not the only one to bring a gift.

It is ended. It is over.

But Michael's eyes open and in the same moment he begins to fade. "Ah, Gina, do you not remember? We have tried this so many times before."

I remember. And once again I wonder what it was we did that condemned my love and me to this strange, tortured, never-ending existence in the outer circle of Hell.

THE SOUND

I. THE SOUND IN WINTER: SYLVIE

We wanted to slip and slide, to fall over and be pulled back onto our feet. We held hands and we laughed. We were going to cross The Sound, to skate across the frozen waves, though our parents had forbidden us this simple pleasure. Like everything else in their grown up world it held too many dangers. They hinted at mysterious perils hidden in deep tidal pools and tried to scare us with tales of others lost to the treacherous sea ice. But we knew better. We had already set our skates on the white surface close to the shore. Today, with the weather set fair and so many hours until sunset, we would have time to venture forth and return before we were even missed.

Robbie and Janice had gone ahead, together as they always were, eighteen and sixteen years wise, testing the path with the broom handle my brother alone had thought to bring. Alison and I, thirteen years young, stayed behind them but not too far. Robbie said if there was a weakness, a warmer current in the water, he wanted to be the one to find it. He would keep his friends and sister safe. No one ever had a better brother than I did.

Half way across he stopped, bent then knelt. Beside him Janice raised her gloved hands to her face and cried out words I couldn't catch. Long seconds passed before she turned and waved to us. "Come, come and look! There's a dead woman under the ice."

My skates dragged on the cold, white surface. I didn't want to see. I wasn't born brave, being more of a cautious soul, taking after my mother. Alison raced ahead of me, impatient for every new sight, each new experience. She stood beside Janice and looked down.

"She's so beautiful." My brother's voice was a hollow whisper. He dragged himself to his feet, using the broom handle for support, on a surface suddenly grown slippery. He raised the wooden pole into the air and brought it crashing down. Splinters of transparent ice rained around his shoulders.

"Stop!" Janice grabbed at his coat.

Oblivious of her, his eyes remained fixed on the woman beneath his feet.

Under me the frozen Sound heaved as though the waves were returning. I looked down into the baleful eye of a large fish. Unmoving, fins fanned, tail spread, it was one of many, an unnatural shoal made up of a dozen different species. Were they dead or were they waiting for something, perhaps something trapped to be released?

The broom handle continued to rise and fall, carving a hole in a surface turning to slush. Janice jumped back, the shards sharp as daggers leaving marks on her face. She reached out but my brother would not let himself be dissuaded from his task. Again the ice heaved and this time a thousand cracks radiated out from the repeated impact of wood on frozen water.

A wavelet raced across my feet. I felt its penetrating cold through my boots and two layers of woollen socks. Fear coursed through me, strong as a surging tide. Unable to stay, I fled toward the shore across the creaking, cracking, now fragmenting ice floes.

Falling, sinking, drowning, treading water too bitter; chilled beyond shivering, my clothing no longer warm, my coat dragged me down among the silver shapes, now swimming past me as they sped toward the woman and my brother.

Alison beside me. "Come on!" Her voice a shiver only a little warmer than the water.

There was sand beneath my fingers, but they were too numb to drag me to safety. It was over. I would be claimed by The Sound, lost with my brother.

Strong arms grasped me, would not let go, and I heard the voice of my mother cajoling me. She hauled me beyond the danger and I landed gasping, clutching at the air on the white rimmed beach beside The Sound. Leaving me, she returned to rescue Alison, though my friend, strong fisherman's daughter that she was, needed no help. Janice flailed her way to join us, her face streaked with icicle tears.

But out in The Sound where no one could reach, there among the miniature icebergs, released from her frozen prison the woman, pale and grey as the sky above us, clasped my brother to her in arms as thin and white as bone. A sound drifted toward us, not Robbie's cries but a strange, swirling, hissing, half-sung song.

A face turned toward us. For a split second I saw crimson eyes as hooded as a viper's, a mouth with too many teeth. Then the woman who was no woman and my brother were both gone, as she took her freedom and her prize, plunging down beneath the white crested waves.

II. THE SOUND IN SPRING: ROBBIE

She was lovely. And she was alive. Janice was wrong to jump away and shout to the others we had found a body in the ice, making them think we had found some poor, frozen corpse. I knew the lady wasn't dead. I could see her lips moving, could hear the faint notes of the song she was singing. Even then I must have known she could not be human but, what was more important to me, I knew she was in trouble; in need of rescue. I raised the broom handle and brought it crashing down. The ice gave up without a fight, splinters spreading in long, jagged lines, a cracked halo around the lady's head.

She rose up from the shards of white water, her arms outstretched, her lips open. Her song was the sound of the sea, of the gulls, of the deeper melodies of time and tide. I did not hear the others leave, saw nothing of my sister's struggle, cared for nothing beyond the notes of the song.

I was captured.

She curled her body around me. It was the embrace of a lover. She curled her song around me. It was the embrace of a trap.

Beneath the ice I felt no cold. I did not fight her. I would have been willing to drown, serenaded to my ending.

But there were others in the water. We were surrounded by fish, more than I had ever seen, more than any net on our fishing boat had ever held. They swam with us, a living carpet of silver scales. My head broke the surface. I breathed, I drifted, all the time a willing captive rocked by small waves, clasped in pale arms, wine-dark hair streaming around me, pale lips beside my ear, a private performance.

We came to a shore. Her sisters seated on jagged rocks, her song blended with theirs becoming all the sounds of the earth, only to cease as she released me. My body lay on rounded pebbles. I had no strength.

She walked from the sea and with each step she changed. No beauty now, her face was a sunken skull ravaged by too much time and too much water, her limbs stick thin, the bones standing out; a carving in relief. "Why have you brought me here before I had finished with him?"

How could such a voice, rasping and cold, come from the same mouth as the song which had beguiled me?

One of the other women raised a hand with crooked fingers, too much bone, too little flesh. "He saved you, Ligeia. He fought the ice and so it is our judgement he has won you. Now you must pay the penalty."

The other sisters nodded in agreement, their fish cold eyes sweeping over me as though assessing me and finding me wanting.

"Seven years is too long."

"It will be over quicker the sooner it is begun."

And so it did begin.

My whole world was the song she sang. Night and morning it was a caress, a thank you for rescue. It was not love, though for five years I believed it was. She lay with me in a nest of soft fern bordered all around with rare treasures from the sea but all the time she was counting the minutes, the hours that made up the days, waiting for the end of the seven years. I think she may have planned to defy her sisters, to drown me when the time came, rather than let me go as custom demanded.

Two years into my captivity we had a daughter. Her cries from the first were an imitation of her mother. She too would be a siren. I had helped create another monster, but knowing what she must become made no difference to me; I loved my child.

Three more years and the next baby was a boy. I saw him only once, a gasping new born refused by his mother. She would not be the parent of something so alien. Men could not be sirens. They were sailors, they were prey. I cried out as her sisters lifted him and took him from our cave. I tried to follow but they evaded me. They lost me as I cut my bare feet to ribbons on the sharp edges of the boulders and scrambled after their receding figures over the cliffs. I do not know what they did with him. Drowned him like some unwanted kitten? I only know the loss of him broke the spell. No man had ever resisted the song before, not even the great Odysseus tied to the mast of his ship. He too had been damaged and ever after there were nights when he wept at the memory of long lost chords. But I, my heart cleaved in two by the loss of a son I had been unable to save, had ears that mourned with the rest of me. Her calling now strident, her music had died.

I tried to pretend but her touch was repulsive. Without the song to blind me, I saw her true shape and now Ligeia was as ancient, ugly and deformed as before she had been young, beautiful and perfect.

Seeking an escape, I took to roaming the island. I judged it to be about a mile across and something like a letter C in shape, though the coast had many inlets, coves and small bays. The sirens' dwellings were clustered on the north side, some living in a collection of huts constructed from bleached driftwood, others preferring to inhabit caves in the tall cliffs. There were, I thought, perhaps ten of them, though it was difficult to be certain as it was rare to see more than two or three together on land at any one time. When they took to the waves they were impossible to count, diving beneath the surface, hair and gowns merging with the water.

As each day slid by, I added to the marks I had been scratching on the wall of my cave. I was determined not to lose track of time. I would never give up the hope of seeing my home and my loved ones again, though I was worried my mind might be failing me. I sometimes imagined I saw boot prints among the sand dunes, traces of a campfire and even a fleeting shadow too broad to be a siren. Once I shouted out but, of course, there was no reply. There could be no one else on this island. The sirens would have dealt with them long ago as I feared they would deal with me if I were still there when the seven years were up.

Ligeia must have sensed my unhappiness, my disenchantment, not that she understood it. Night and morning, as she continued to sing, I closed my eyes and thought about my home.

After a while she told me our daughter was to spend less time with me. Tiny though she might be, she said, the girl must learn the ways of her people, be brought up to know the notes of the song. I disagreed but it was useless. I woke the next morning alone in the cave, mother and daughter both gone. I had wanted her to leave but not like this.

Three days later she returned and reminded me there were two more years to go before our contract would be dissolved. She said there was still time for another daughter, she would come to me often. I told her to go back to her sisters. I wanted no more children. I saw the confusion in her eyes as she sang. Even so, I stood in the mouth of the cave barring her from it and my bed.

A month or so later a fishing boat sailed too close to the island. I could do nothing for the crew, four young men standing at the rail, eyes wide at the sight of the beauty bobbing in the sea, minds captured by the song swelling around them. They fought each other for the privilege of being the first to dive into the water. They had no idea it was only the privilege of being the first to drown in the storm summoned by the sirens.

The boat survived. I boarded the Esmerelda and steered her into the tiny cove beside the cave. I hid her as best I could and began to stock her with provisions transferred from other wrecks around the island. One ancient vessel had been half beached for what must have been centuries. In the hold I found a large chest with rare contents. It took me three trips to stow everything. Then I waited.

Weeks later, on a fine, clear moonlit night, while they were distracted with the drowning of another set of victims, I set sail, steering around the island until I was certain the cliffs concealed me from their view. From there I had no idea which way to go but I had provisions for at least a month and I was a good sailor. I knew the sirens would not want to let me go but I also knew, until the seven years were up, they would not harm me. I looked back only once. I would miss my daughter. I breathed my farewell into the wind, along with a promise; if there was any way to rescue her, I would find it.

III. THE SOUND IN SUMMER: SYLVIE

Five years after we had lost him, my brother Robbie returned to us. I was eighteen and a lot had happened since the cold winter day when four of us had set off to skate across the frozen Sound. There had been an accident: the ice had cracked. Alison, Janice and I had made it back to the shore but Robbie, who had been ahead of us, had drowned. Or at least that was what we thought had happened. Yet here he was standing on our doorstep, looking a little older, dressed in an outlandish suit which would have been more at home in a costume drama.

I had been ill for a while after the accident. I would wake, crying, from strange dreams in which Robbie was being kidnapped by a mermaid which he had released from the ice. Of course, since there is no such thing as mermaids, they had to be dreams, though they felt more like memories. I asked the other two what they thought had happened on that day. Alison claimed to remember less than I did, while Janice refused to speak of it at all, though from time to time I would catch her gazing out into The Sound, her eyes filled with tears. I was not the only one who missed my brother.

Around us the shoreline was becoming ever more deserted. Several people left after a couple of strong storms swamped our houses and it became clear the village would be lost to the sea within a few years. But our three families, bound together in tragedy and in our love of the coast, were determined to stay where we were until forced to move. "We won't go until there are fish swimming on the carpet," was the way my father put it.

Robbie gave an explanation of what had happened to him. I didn't believe the tale he told and I was sure my parents didn't either. He said he had come close to freezing to death in the icy sea before being picked up by a trawler. He had lost his memory and by the time he had recovered it he was half way round the world. He had liked the life so much he had decided to stay on as part of the crew. Even so, he was sorry for all the hurt he must have caused by disappearing. This statement led to a row which shook the walls. A week later my mother was still not speaking to him.

He agreed to move out and took up residence in one of the empty cottages. It was an odd choice because part of the building had already fallen into the sea and at high tide the waves filled what had been the kitchen.

It was early in the morning when I sneaked out of the house to go and see him. I hoped my parents would forgive him soon but, with no sign of any reconciliation yet, I went without telling them.

The front door was open. I called out his name as I entered but there was no reply. I decided he must have gone out for a walk and so made my way into the lounge to wait for him. In the centre of the room was a huge wooden chest. It looked for all the world like one of those you see in illustrations in children's books about pirates. I couldn't help myself. I had to know what was inside.

The lid was heavy, the wood smooth as if it had been polished, though it was dull, not shiny. It opened with a loud creak and I was looking at a large pile of old clothes. Disappointed, I wrinkled my nose at the strong salt smell coming from the cream linen shirt. It had frilled lace at the neck, like an elaborate blouse. Beneath it was a much more modern pair of blue jeans and a polo shirt. Two thick, woollen jumpers came next, one plain green, the other a hand knitted Fair Isle. Beneath them were several t-shirts and pairs of modern boxer shorts. It was an odd collection. I realised my brother must have been using the chest as a suitcase.

I had still to reach the bottom of the box. As I raised the last t-shirt my mouth fell open. The clothes had been laid on top of a layer of money. There were pounds, euros, dollars and half a dozen other currencies all tied together in neat, thick bundles. No one could have earned this much working on a trawler. What had my brother really been doing? Was he a robber? A drug runner? I ought to have put the clothes back and left but there was something else glinting beneath the banknotes. I laid them on the carpet and sat back on my heels as I stared down at the final contents of the chest. There were at least a hundred coins. They looked old and mixed up, all different sizes and shapes, but I was certain they had one thing in common: they were all made of gold.

"Ah, so you've found them."

I turned my head. Robbie was standing in the doorway watching me.

"Where did you get them from?"

"I found them. It took me a while to collect so many but don't worry, sis, they're all mine. I didn't steal them. Well, not in the way you would recognise as stealing."

"What do you mean? Either you stole them or you didn't."

He ran a hand over his mouth. "It's a long story."

"Like the one you told Mum and Dad?"

"No, this one's true. The coins and the notes belonged to my wife so, in a way, they do belong to me."

"Your wife? You got married?"

"Yeah, sort of. But not in a way our parents would accept."

"Where is she? Hasn't she come with you?"

"She can't and, if she could, I wouldn't want her to. I've spent the last five years trying to get away from her and her people."

"You've been held prisoner?"

He sat down in the centre of the old, threadbare settee. "It's difficult to escape when you're in a cave on a tiny island surrounded by the sea."

"I don't understand. How did you get to an island? Did the trawler crew dump you there?"

"Oh, Sylvie, listen to yourself. I thought you understood there was never any trawler. Don't you remember what happened that day on The Sound and the woman I found trapped in the ice?"

His words reopened the door I had tried to keep tight shut inside my mind. "I remember, but Robbie..."

He closed his eyes for a moment. "I broke the ice with the broom handle. I couldn't stop. I couldn't leave her. She was so lovely. Even if she had been dead, I couldn't have left her there."

I shook my head. What was he talking about? "There was no lovely woman. I saw what happened to you as I lay on the beach. You were tangled up with a skeleton, all pale bone and..." I bit my lip, unwilling to say the words, the impossible words. "It had eyes like a snake and teeth... No lips but so many long, curved teeth."

"You saw the truth. You saw her as she is, not as the song she sings makes her appear." He reached out and grasped my arm. "You wouldn't have heard the song. Most women don't. While I was on the island, she and her sisters lured so many boats to them. The men on the vessels dived into the sea. They didn't fight. They saw only beauty and couldn't think of anything but the song in their ears. If there were women on board, most of them heard nothing and saw what you did. Their deaths were much harder but they still drowned in the end."

I struggled free from him and stood back. "You're describing a siren but they don't exist. They can't exist. They're nothing but a myth."

"I only wish that were true." He turned away from me and scooped up a handful of the coins from the chest. "I took these from some of the ships they had sunk, dead men's treasure, and the boat I sailed into the harbour belonged to a crew they drowned last month."

It was strange but I did not doubt him. "What are you going to do? We have to tell everyone what happened to you."

"We can't. I have no proof. Besides, the world must not know about them. They're too dangerous. Imagine the havoc their song could cause if it were broadcast. The beaches would be full of men trying to take to the sea, the cliffs a route for mass suicide. They make you want to swim to them, no matter how impossible that may be. No, I came back to try to find a way to fight them, perhaps even find help."

"I don't think that's a good idea. It's too risky. You should forget them. You have all this money and your own little boat in the harbour. Stay close to shore. Fish! Stay with us, Robbie."

"I can't do that either." He drew in a noisy breath. "I have to go back. I have to rescue Maya, my daughter."

Once I had recovered from the shock of discovering I had a niece who was half siren, I told him he would not have to deal with his problem alone any longer. I would not allow him to sail into danger without my help. We would restock the Esmerelda and be ready to leave in a few days. Although he tried to protest, I could see the relief in his eyes.

I ought to have known it would be impossible to keep our friends from finding out we were preparing for a long voyage. Janice's father worked in the chandler's store and orders as large as ours were not common.

A couple of days before our planned departure, when Robbie and I arrived at the Esmerelda, we discovered the other two waiting for us in the cabin. They had been to the house and found the trunk.

Janice tossed a handful of gold coins onto the table. They landed with a harsh metallic clinking.

Robbie tried to bluster her with a tale of treasure hunting but I interrupted with the truth. For a while they didn't believe but, when I reminded them of the woman in the ice, it was as though their doubts crumbled and dispersed like the walls of a sandcastle besieged by a neap tide. Both of them insisted on coming with us.

Janice took hold of his hand. "I've waited five years for you to come back to me. Do you think I'm going to let you disappear on your own again?"

Alison pointed out they were good sailors, hardy and used to life on the shoreline. Besides, they were women and hadn't Robbie said women were immune to the song of the sirens?

It was a short discussion.

We set sail with no clear plan, only a determination to rescue Robbie's daughter. Something would turn up.

Robbie was a good sailor and a careful navigator. He had kept a log as he made his way home to us. The Esmerelda was not a sophisticated vessel. Her original voyage with the four young sailors who had drowned could not have been a long one. There was no radio and only a rudimentary set of charts.

It took us two months to find a landmark Robbie recognised. Once he was sure the mountain on the horizon was the one in the centre of the sirens' island, we made for another nearby shore. We restocked with fruit and fresh water. We wanted to be ready to make our escape. Even so, we still had no clear plan.

We decided to spend the night ashore. The sand was warm, soft and golden. We brought blankets from the boat in anticipation of the temperature dropping but the breeze remained tropical. I was too hot and after a while of tossing and turning gave up trying to sleep and instead took a walk along the beach.

I had not gone far when I made out a figure. Someone was standing calf deep in the sea. Was this a siren? Had we already been discovered?

I was about to run for the others when a snatch of song reached me. The voice was soft and lyrical, nothing like the discordant cacophony Robbie had described.

After a moment I recognised the singer. "Alison? What are you doing?"

She turned from the waves to look at me. "I wonder what it must be like to be a siren, to be so lovely."

"Lovely? What makes you say that? You saw the one who took Robbie. She was like a skeleton: all teeth and bones."

"No, I suppose you're right. Not lovely at all." She waded back to me. "Come on. Let's get some rest. Tomorrow will be a big day."

I trailed after her, unable to shake the feeling something was amiss. Could Alison have some sympathy for our foes?

IV. THE SOUND IN AUTUMN: ROBBIE

It was a relief when Sylvie told me she believed me about the sirens. I hadn't realised she had seen me being dragged beneath the waves. At first I was unsure about also bringing Janice and Alison along on the voyage to rescue my daughter. I didn't want to place them in any danger but after a few days I realised they were just as capable of sailing the Esmerelda and were as strong as I was. They had the added advantage of also being female and therefore immune to the sirens' deadly singing. I could not have chosen better companions.

We sailed for some time until the day I spotted a familiar island on the horizon. With the binoculars in my hand, I froze and stared across the wine-dark sea. For a split second I wanted to turn the boat around. I had not expected to feel so afraid. There were still over thirteen long months to go until the end of the seven years but would Ligeia and the other sirens still feel bound to keep their bargain? Had my sailing away from them overturned their obligation to keep me safe? Would I be able to resist them or would my ears betray me? I thought of my daughter held in their tender care, being taught to hate all men, to see them as nothing more than prey. Whatever the risks, I could not allow Maya to become a pale copy of her mother.

On the eve of our rescue attempt we sat together in the cabin. We argued on how to tackle the sirens. Alison was in favour of threatening them with the guns we had brought. Sylvie said she wasn't sure they would be harmed even if we did shoot them. She was afraid they might be immortal. I, knowing whatever they were, there was little human about them, agreed with her.

Alison became angry, insisting it was worth the risk.

"There is only one thing we can do." Janice tapped the table, bringing the argument to a close. "We stay out of sight among the wrecks in the bay until they do spot us, then we distract them; give them a target. We sail the Esmerelda close in but not too close. If we wear oilskins and sou'westers, they won't be able to tell we're not men. They won't know they can't affect us so they'll leave the island in pursuit. We will stay just out of reach while you get your daughter."

I didn't like the idea. "It's too risky. I've seen them drown women too. They're fast in the water, faster than dolphins."

Alison changed sides. "Oh, I don't know. It might work. This boat isn't slow in the water either. It will take them a while to realise there are no men aboard and perhaps you could set their homes on fire or something so they have to stop chasing us and go back."

I was outnumbered, my reservations ignored as the three of them refined their plan. They were sure my daughter would not be among the adults. The sirens would have to leave her ashore since she was still a toddler and too young to take part in the action. I had my doubts and even if they were right, would she be left on the shore alone?

When we reached the point where the island was less than a mile away, the time came for me to make my decision. I did not want to leave the three of them to face the sirens. Their lack of knowledge worried me but I would never have a better chance. It was now or never.

As I was lowering the dinghy into the water from the prow of the Esmerelda, Sylvie strode up to me. "I'm coming with you."

"No, our friends will need your help. I can deal with this."

"Can you? Where's the rope? And don't forget you'll need some cloth to gag her with."

"What are you talking about?"

"A three year old child who hardly knows you, do you believe she'll let you pick her up, stuff her under your arm like a parcel and carry her away from her mother without any fuss? Why should she? You're a stranger. She'll scream and struggle. Can you row the dinghy and keep hold of her at the same time?"

She was right. I hadn't thought about Maya's likely reaction. Even before I escaped from the island all I saw of her was a small figure in the distance holding onto her mother's hand. I had no choice. I made way for Sylvie and she scrambled down the rope ladder and grasped the oars. "I'll take us in, you bring us out."

I looked up at the rail. Janice smiled at me. "Go on, fetch her. Don't worry about us. Alison and I can manage. You can do this. You'll soon be back."

I wished I shared her confidence in me.

It didn't take long to reach the outcrop of jagged rocks surrounding the natural harbour from which I had sailed. Beaching the dinghy on the narrow strip of pebbles, we hid it among the scattered boulders.

Above us towered the cliff, but the climb to the cave was not difficult. The path had been trodden often enough. Sylvie and I could be there in seconds but if someone was inside, we would be seen.

I was about to suggest she let me go on alone when the air was rent by raucous cries, hideous screeches and rasping discords. The sirens were singing. It could mean only one thing: the Esmerelda had been spotted.

Our friends were in danger.

Before we could react, there was another disturbance.

"Not this time."

"Mama, please!"

Sylvie and I ducked behind boulders as Ligeia strode past us, so close I could have touched her. But all her attention was on dragging our child, who was in the throes of a violent tantrum.

She lifted the girl off her feet. "Be quiet! Do as you're told." The sound of her hand slapping our daughter's face was followed by more crying.

At that exact second came a series of loud bangs, the unmistakeable sound of gunfire. If Janice and Alison had already resorted to using the weapons, they had to be in trouble.

Maya howled as her mother swung her higher. "Come on. Don't be difficult." They vanished into the cave.

I was torn. Should I go after my daughter or race to the beach? I had brought everyone into such peril. The sirens were so strong; much stronger and more dangerous than any mortal.

Another salvo of gunfire, another cacophony of discord. My dilemma solved itself as Ligeia emerged from the cave. She rushed down the narrow path to the sea, scattering small stones in her haste. Was it possible Alison was right? Could bullets harm the sirens?

Hoping it was so, I took my chance. I left Sylvie as lookout and pushed open the door into my former prison.

My daughter, her eyes wide, blinked at me.

"It's all right, Maya. It's Daddy. I've come to save you."

She cowered back against the damp wall of the cave, her shoulder brushing the marks I had carved. She was trembling. Sylvie was right. My daughter did not know me and Maya would not be the name the sirens called her.

I scooped her up.

She began to struggle but she was not strong and her previous tantrum had worn her out.

With Sylvie just in front, I scrambled with Maya down to the dinghy. As we headed into the waves, my daughter wriggled and squirmed, trying to clamber over the side, but my sister encased her in her arms.

"It's all right, Maya. Let's go and find mummy, shall we?"

I might not have liked it but it was the right thing to say. Maya settled into a sullen silence, her large, green eyes scanning the waves.

The dinghy rounded the headland. In a few seconds we would be in open water. I held my breath, afraid at any moment we would be spotted and the sirens would turn their attention to us. We were taking their most precious possession from them. And we had no defence.

But the waves were empty: no sign of shapes speeding through the water, no cacophony of recognition. Nothing.

"Where have they gone?"

"I don't know, Sylvie. Back to the shore maybe." I couldn't work it out. How could the chase already be over? "And where's the Esmerelda? She couldn't have sunk so quickly, not without leaving any trace. There's not even any debris on the surface."

"What about over there?" Sylvie pointed to the tangle of wrecks further out in the bay: more craft than I could count, small fishing boats, medium sized trawlers and two ancient galleons; all deserted, their crews having been willing victims of the sirens. Many more ships were sunk below the waves. Here and there I could make out a crows nest atop a lost mast. The water was choppy, broken up by the many wooden reefs close beneath the surface.

To find a safe passage through this unseen labyrinth would have taken more skill than I possessed.

But Sylvie was adamant the Esmerelda could have made her way through. "Jan is the best sailor on the coast. She has her own craft now.

She fishes the sandbanks and shoals in The Sound and she's never run aground."

I tried to say this was different but I hoped Sylvie was right.

The dinghy was small and had a shallow enough draught to skim over the water between the wrecks. If the Esmerelda was among them, she had to be close to the galleons. Anywhere else and she would be visible to us.

And to the sirens.

The passage between the two mighty vessels was narrow. Their sides, glistening with seaweed and encrusted by barnacles, towered over us.

From one of them a long rope ladder trailed into the sea. It looked new, out of place against the ancient timbers. It had not come from the Esmerelda but could our friends have found it and made use of it?

Securing the dinghy to the bottom rung, we began the long and challenging climb, the ladder swinging outward and back. Maya struggled and I almost dropped her, but at last we reached the deck.

I leaned on an old cannon, thick with verdigris, while I got my breath back. If our friends were here, there was no sign of them. I shouted their names, while Sylvie wandered over toward the stern.

"Look at this." She was standing by another pair of cannon. Sandwiched between them was a modern winch and a small motor boat. "There must be someone else here."

I remembered the prints on the beach, which had been made by boots, not the naked feet of sirens, the shadow I had glimpsed more than once and the traces of a fire at the base of the cliff.

"So, found yer way 'ere, did yer?" A man was standing a few feet away. He must have crept up on us while we were examining his boat.

"Yes but we didn't know there was anyone aboard. We're looking for our friends."

He stared at me. His intense gaze made me uncomfortable. "Two women, was it?"

"That's right. On a small boat. Do you know where they are?"

"Nah. They jumped off when it got caught up in't fishing nets, over there by that trawler. Swam away, they did. Could be anywhere by now."

I followed his finger. The Esmerelda was not far from us. She floated, silent on the water. If she were snarled up below the surface, I couldn't see it. But that didn't mean it wasn't true.

"You're sure the sirens didn't get them?"

Ignoring Sylvie's question, the man continued to stare at me. "You shouldn't 'ang around. Them sirens don't care to come 'ere as a rule. Nothin' for 'em, see. But all that'll change now." He jerked his chin towards Maya. "That's their little girl, innit? They'll want 'er back. Treat 'er like a princess, they do."

"She's my daughter. I came to rescue her."

He snorted. "Made a bit of a mess of that, 'aven't yer? Best thing you can do is go back where yer came from."

Sylvie protested and again he did not react. It was as though...

"You're deaf, aren't you?"

"Yep and a good job I am too. I'd 'ave been dead ages ago if I'd been able to 'ear their song."

"How long have you been here, er, Mister...?"

"George. Call me George and I've no idea but it's been a long time. Them monsters drowned my son and sank 'is boat. And there were nowt I could do about it." He heaved a sigh. "At first I moved around a lot, tried to keep ahead of 'em. But they've given up on me. It's live and let live now."

"I'm sorry about your son. But we have to find our friends. Sylvie and I can't leave without them. Can you help us?"

"Well, I'd say yer don't 'ave time for that. They'll come looking fer't little 'un and I don't see 'em givin' up easy."

Sylvie touched him on the arm. "If you do help Robbie and me, we can get you out of here. There'd be room on the Esmerelda. Don't you want to go home?"

"'Course I wanna leave but I don't see 'ow I can 'elp yer. Like I said, yer mates could be anywhere." He swept his hand over the graveyard of ships. "Even on't island by now. There's loads of rowin' boats, dinghies and the like. They won't 'ave 'ad to swim far."

He was right. Within a short distance of the galleon there had to be more than a hundred wrecks. It would take weeks to search them all. Nor could we afford to attract attention to us in the hope Janice or Alison would see our signal. By now Ligeia would have discovered her loss. She and her sisters would be out hunting for us.

If I wanted to keep my daughter, I had to accept I could not help our comrades. But how could I leave them with no hope of escape?

George was watching me. He coughed. "Listen, young Robbie, I can wait to go 'ome. I want to 'urt them creatures like they've 'urt me. They took my child. Someone should take theirs. Go. I'll find your friends. Then between us we'll look fer another boat and follow yer 'ome."

He would not be dissuaded. He gave me a push towards the motor boat. We set out for the Esmerelda and it was the work of an hour to disentangle her.

Before we left for home, George had one last thing to show us. He led us down into the belly of the galleon. We entered a cabin. No doubt it had belonged to the captain. What had once been expensive brocade on the furnishings was now a tattered mass of salt encrusted rags. There were several chests grouped together beside what would have been the bed.

He flung open the lid of the nearest. Gold does not tarnish no matter how long it has been in salt water. Gems sparkle no matter how long they lie in a decaying wooden box. Riches remain riches. Here on this galleon was a fortune.

"Yer should take some of this back with yer."

He didn't need to make the suggestion twice.

The chests were too heavy to move. We recovered only about a quarter and even had we taken it all, the cabin held only a fraction of the treasure on this one ship.

George helped us transfer onto the Esmerelda as much as we believed we could carry without compromising her seaworthiness.

We were unhappy at the prospect of leaving him and our friends behind and we might have delayed longer, perhaps risked a search of the nearest wrecks, but, as we stood together on the deck, I heard a sound in the water.

I rushed to the rail and caught a glimpse of one of the sirens heading through the waves back towards the island.

Soon they would all know where we were.

We scrambled down the rope ladder. George headed off in the motor boat while Sylvie, Maya and I set the Esmerelda's sails and made for the open sea.

Eight days out, we encountered a terrible storm. Despite our best efforts we were forced to surrender our vessel to the sea. Perhaps we had overloaded her after all.

For two further days we were tossed on huge waves in our tiny lifeboat before having the good fortune to be rescued by a trawler.

And so we arrived home. The only treasure we were able to salvage was a necklace Sylvie had taken for herself and was wearing when we were picked up. Look. Here it is. See how the diamonds sparkle.

Since then we have spent every waking moment watching the sea. But three months have passed and there is no sign of Janice, Alison or George.

They are the reason I am here tonight. I am asking for your help. I must return to the island. I refuse to abandon that brave man and my good friends. I cannot leave them to the mercy of the sirens. I believe there is still hope for them. They are strong and resourceful people.

All I ask of you is a little financial assistance: enough to buy a larger boat, equip it with everything required for the voyage and to arm a small group to aid me in this rescue. You will not only be saving three lives but you will also be well compensated, since we will not return empty handed. Besides bringing George and the women home, we will return with a hold filled with treasure stolen by the sirens.

Think of it. You can be a hero: save three lives and make a fortune at the same time. What better way to invest your money could there possibly be?

MEET DENARII PETERS

Denarii Peters is lost among the fens and the wolds of East Anglia and Lincolnshire. It's taken her a long time to get there. If needed she can be found gazing into the distance, over her computer keyboard, with a cup of coffee in one hand.

In a previous life she did many things; worked in several different offices: a communications company, a steel distributors, a maker of artificial limbs and she logged colours for a dyeing company. Later she became a primary school teacher and had two children of her own. She lived in many northern places: from Lancaster to Bradford then, with her husband, spent five years travelling all over Western Europe towing a caravan.

She has always told stories: to her friends, to the children she taught and then, after a lot of encouragement, she began to write them down.

Now she can't stop. Fortunately and rather to her surprise, over the last two years she has found success in more than fifty short story and flash fiction competitions both in Britain and abroad. Nothing makes her happier than knowing someone, somewhere is enjoying her scribblings.

You can catch up with her latest stories and books on Substack here: https://denariipeters.substack.com/

SNEAK A PEEK

.. at Denarii's latest work in progress, The Reluctant Reaper. Due out in April 2025. Sign up for news at www.crystalclearbooks.co.uk.

CHAPTER 1

That last shot came far too close, spattering my face with cold, slimy mud. As I crawled through gorse, thorns a thousand prickling points of pain, my clutching fingers tore at scrubby grass on the edge of the abyss. I cried out as a nail ripped free.

With nothing but unresisting air beneath my other hand, I fell over the precipice; one more sad ghost to wail in the wind whistling around Greystone Crags.

Tumbling, falling; clothes snagging on sharp shards of granite, I wrapped my arms around my head and bounced like a cannon ball down a mountain, crashing into boulders; drowning in an ocean of pain.

My eyes opened to a pale sky arching above me. Dawn: cold, damp but still alive, I lay on my back at the foot of the crag.

How could I have survived such an impossible fall? I held my hands up in front of my face, turning them over and over. Nothing more than a dozen deep scratches, a missing nail, bruises and a few drops of dried blood: almost no damage at all.

Laughing out loud, I hugged the rocks as I hauled myself to my feet; breathed a sigh of relief as my legs held me. Every muscle ached, but no worse than I had endured in the past falling from a horse.

What a shame there was no one around to tell about my remarkable escape. Ah yes, it was indeed an escape. But was I safe? What had happened to my pursuers? Had my tumble down the cliff convinced Elias Robertshaw and his men I was dead?

Even if it had, I couldn't stay where I was. Once the light was strong enough they would search the base of the cliff for my body. If they were to discover I was still alive, my miraculous escape would have all been for nothing. They would arrest me, try me and hang me. I was a wanted man: an important fugitive. The bounty on my head would keep the thirstiest man in ale for months.

I had to find somewhere out of the way to hide up. This part of the country was getting far too hot for me. Last night I had come within a whisker of getting caught. Should I consider moving on? Well, it wouldn't be easy. I was only familiar with the roads in this area and it's difficult to be a successful highwayman if you're not acquainted with the highways.

My best option would be to make my way to an inn where I hoped they would give me a friendly reception. It was a fair way off so I would have to get a move on.

Keeping an eye out for any pursuit, I clambered over the rocky terrain until I reached the edge of the dusty road which led away from the cliffs.